THE TIME HAS COME

Alfonso Fumero

THE TIME HAS COME

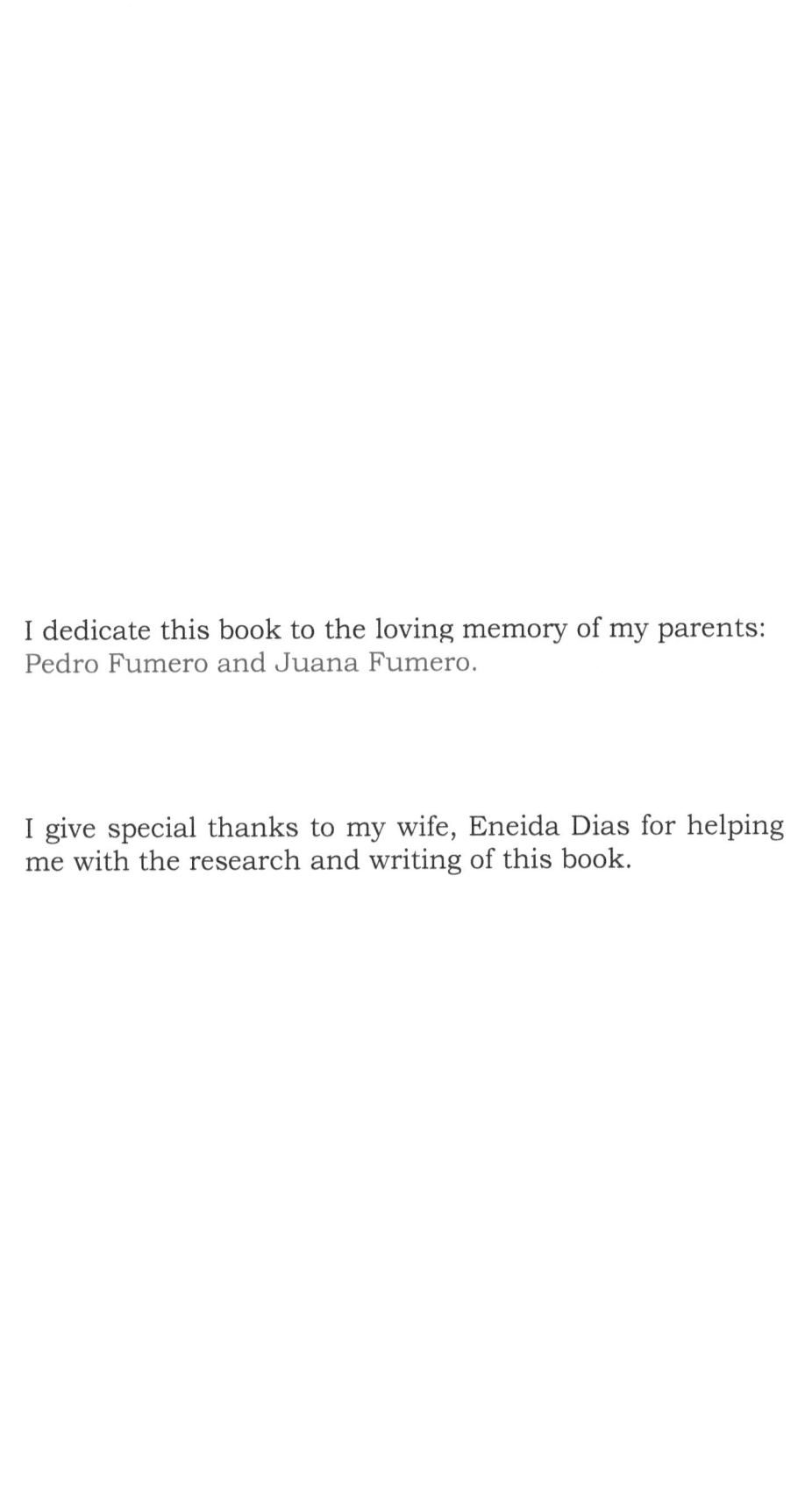

I dedicate this book to the loving memory of my parents: Pedro Fumero and Juana Fumero.

I give special thanks to my wife, Eneida Dias for helping me with the research and writing of this book.

For nations shall rise against nations, and kingdoms against kingdoms: And there shall be earthquakes in diverse places, And there shall be famine and troubles: these are the beginnings of sorrows.

–Mark 13:8

PROLOGUE

It was a very cold night in a remote wooded area in Bosnia. The wind blew very aggressively as it howled among the dead trees of the frozen forest. The snow continuously fell without ceasing as it became part of the snow already sitting three feet deep on the ground. The skies were covered with thick gray clouds which assured that there was no end nearing to the storm. Behind the clouds sat a full moon shining as a beacon, announcing a message of doom unseen by mortal eyes. For the light of the powerful full moon would never penetrate the depth of the monstrous gray clouds.

In the middle of this solitary area, full of death and cold sat a log cabin. From the stone chimney escaped smoke showing the only sign of life in the area. Inside a woman laid on the bed yelling and screaming as sweat ran down her face and body. Another older woman was between her legs trying to help her give birth, as a younger woman ran back and forth with pots and pales of hot water. Blood was all over the old bed and sheets, as the woman's screams echoed in the silence of the storm.

Two bearded men with coats stood by the door watching intensely, but not saying a word.

"Vruca Voda!" The lady delivering the baby yelled.

"Rucnici! Zuriti!" The same lady continued to yell as she was delivering the baby.

As the younger lady ran back and forth getting pots of hot water and towels. Then there was a loud scream that ripped through the silence of the forest; and seconds later the cry of a new born.

"Gotovo je! Dje cak je!!" The older lady helping to give birth yelled, as the crying of a baby boy was heard. The older lady held the baby boy in a blanket as the room glowed with the light from the fire.

The two men walked to the women and one of the men took the baby in his arms. The woman that gave birth looked at the men with wide eyes and desperation.

"Moja beba! Moja beba!" She yelled, "My baby" in Croatian. The other bearded man looked at her as he took out a gun, pointed it at her face and as the lady screamed he shot her in the head. The other two women looked in horror, but before they were able to react, the man shot them both in the head. The man with the gun made sure all three women were dead. Then in a split second the two men left with the baby bundled into the night. The man with the gun set the cabin on fire. As they entered a vehicle prepared for excess snow, the cabin was left behind burning to ashes.

CHAPTER ONE

The New World Order

Jill walked slowly into the cold, concrete and glass government building. She opened the heavy glass door and walked towards the metal detectors where three guards, without expression, stood with rifles. One of the guards silently pointed to the rail by the metal detector. The light skin bony hand of the young lady placed her small handbag on the rail. She walked through the metal detector and found two other guards with rifles on the other side. Jill's eyes nervously roamed around trying to observe and understand as much as she could about her surroundings. As she picked up her bag off the rail, she showed the letter she had received from the United State government a week ago to one of the guards. The guard glanced at it, and pointed towards the two heavy oak doors without a word. As Jill walked towards the doors she could hear the echo of her heals clacking on the marble floors. It was a cold sound and she felt a very uneasy hollow feeling within her chest, as she wondered what has happened to her nation, "the Land of the Free".

Slowly, she opened the doors and found a big room full of people, wall to wall. On the front side of the room there were small windows with bullet proof glass like the tellers at a bank. Some people were standing and others were sitting on the cold marble floors, but they were all lined-up in front of the tellers. The young woman realized that there were about twenty of these tellers and there were a few hundred people in this room. For a second, she thought about leaving. But she remembered the bold black letters in the letter from the United States Government,

"Not keeping your appointment will be considered as an act of treason towards the United States Government and will be dealt with accordingly."

Jill took a deep breath and walked towards the back of the room. She was grateful for the sun light that came through the big office windows that were uniformly spread on the wall. The windows were closed but there was a comfortable cool air coming through the vents. Unfortunately, there were so many people that you couldn't help feeling a bit claustrophobic. The room was lit very brightly and the walls were painted white with two large flat screens at each side of the room. They tried to make the room cheerful and as comfortable as possible, but she did not appreciate the reason for having to be there.

As Jill walked past the people she heard a lot of whispering. People were talking to each other but no one was being loud. She could not tell if they were being respectful or motivated by fear. She saw men and women, young and old, as well as children, many types of people all with the same look, confused and uncertain. They did not know what to expect. They had many unanswered questions. The future seemed uncertain. The future was here. It meant that radical changes were a curing in our country and in our life style, and we did not have a choice. Some very *intelligent* people decided what would be *good* for us.

Jill realized by now that she was not sure where to go. She saw a short lady, who had black hair with a gray streak, wearing a black raincoat, caught her attention. Her eyes looked smart and energetic, she felt safe speaking to her.

"Excuse me, how do I find out where to go?" Jill asked the short lady.

The short lady with the dark energetic eyes spoke to her with a big smile, "All the letters are alike, Dear. If you look on the top right side of your letter you will see a long number with eight digits. Find where your number fits with the numbers over the windows and that's your teller. That will be your line."

"Thank you."

"Sure, sweetheart. Good luck."

The short lady spoke with so much energy. Jill realized that some people did not mind being here. She wondered if this spunky intelligent lady knew something she didn't. If all people were being treated the same, if this was finally equality for all, why did it feel so wrong? She found her place and feeling like a sheep, she quietly stood in line.

In front of her stood a young pregnant woman, she seemed tired and pale. She was thin and her face looked dehydrated.

"Are you ok? Can I get you anything?" Jill asked her.

"No, thank you," she answered as she turned around to face Jill and continue to rub her belly. "It's the pregnancy and I feel jumpy with everything that's going on." As she spoke she looked at the door nervously as when someone is speaking to you, but their mind is somewhere else.

Jill looked at the pregnant girl with empathy, "Well, try to relax. My name is Jill. If I could help you let me know." Jill said with a smile.

The pregnant girl looked at her and giving-in to Jill's hospitality consented to answer, "Hi, my name is Deborah," as she forced a smile.

"When are you due?" Jill asked, as she thank God that she was not the one who was pregnant. She does not want to pass through that again, especially at these times.

Deborah looked at her tired; as she answered, "In three months. That's the real reason I am here. I am so tired of this, that I don't care anymore about who is right or who is wrong. All I know is that if I don't get the Micro Biochip I will not be able to continue with my check-ups, my doctor will not continue to treat me and no hospital will even except me to deliver my baby. I don't care about doing this, but I have to."

Jill agreed with Deborah and nodded with understanding. Jill added with anger, "To that you have to add, that you will not be able to buy anything at the supermarket or any store. I am a single parent of a four year old boy I need food and clothes for my little boy. I don't want a foreign object in my body, but what is a person supposed to do?"

"What has happen to our country?" Jill continued, "If we do not have this chip in our hand we will be like outcasts from our own society. We will not be able to drive, to buy anything or get medical help. *The Christians* are saying that this is wrong. They are talking about the number of the beast and the end of times. It all sounds scary and crazy."

When Jill mentioned the Christians Deborah looked at her and her eyes watered. She fought back her tears as to not cry as she listened to Jill.

"I don't see any Christian knocking at my door to help me feed my little boy. I don't know how those Christians are going to survive. I have a Christian brother, he refuses to put the chip on, and he is out there with nothing. He was begging me not to come here today. But I am here with my letter and I will do the best for my son and me."

Jill realized that Deborah was tired and more concerned with looking towards the door. Jill felt bad; Deborah seemed as jumpy as a squirrel and decided to end the conversation. She was afraid that the conversation was making her nervous. As Jill stood there in silence she began to listen to some of the people around her. A tall man in his fifty's, wearing a suite, he either had to be a lawyer or businessman was carrying on about how great this chip will be. "I am so excited. With this chip we will be able to travel with ease and I will be able to access my accounts around the world without a bankcard. It will even make easier to get into my Mercedes with my hand just touching the car window. I won't have to worry about hackers getting the numbers of my credit cards on the streets. I guess we only have to worry about them stealing the chip out our skin." He laughed loudly at his own joke. The young lady wrinkled her forehead, not sure if she understood the businessman. Then she heard an older lady behind her whose husband was dying of cancer and she needed him to continue to receive his chemotherapy, without the chip the therapy will be "discontinued", the letter said. She was hoping to fix the matter. All around her there was a world of endless stories and situations; she didn't want to hear anymore.

At that moment everyone became deathly silent as they saw the screens come to life with a video of the President of the United States. It was a recording made by the President to be played specifically for the citizens getting the chip.

"My fellow Americans, as your President it is with great honor that I congratulate you for coming forth on this day and placing a "Biochip" in your hand and becoming a true American Citizen who is ready to go forward into the future of a free nation and opening the doors of opportunities of a new world solidification. As a nation we have gone through some very difficult turmoil economically, politically, as well as experiencing natural disasters. But we are uniting with our European Allies in a way that the "New World" solidification and the Biochip will help us all to grow into a stable world financially as well as technologically. We will find ourselves in a safe and productive future.

With this Biochip you will have better control of your life and your finances. You will be able to enjoy more easily your money as well as pay your bills. With the Biochip you will be able to feel at ease, knowing that your children cannot be taken from you. With the Biochip you will be able to travel across borders around the world with ease and yet feel safe, that the times of terrorists, bombings and the killing of innocent people have come to a halt. I understand that change could sometimes be difficult and even scary; but the future is here today and we are ready to move into a better world.

I know that there are Christians, who are being extreme fanatics and are against the Biochip. They refer to the Chip as "the Number of the Beast", "Satanical", and "the end of the world as we know it". Fear and ignorance are the enemies of progress and we, the greatest nation in the world, cannot partake or give in to fear and ignorance. As President of the United States I only hope that our Christian brothers will one day realize the benefits of these changing times and be a part of our bright future. Today you become part of a new America, a New World and a new era in this nation's great history. Thank you and I congratulate you."

When the speech ended many people started to clap and cheer loudly showing their support for the President and their country. Some were quiet not sure what to say and many were quite verbal in showing their displeasure towards this obligated process that was being forced upon American citizens. It was quite scary and intense. Children in the room hung on tight to their parents with fear, as they innocently followed their parent's decision to be there.

One man stood tall as he began to yell over all the other voices and the room became silent to hear him, "You generation of vipers! You have no right to force your perverted and coerced plans into our personal bodies. This is anti-American and you are staining the words of our "Constitution", trampling over our freedom and degrading the idealisms of the fathers of this nation. You are slapping the face of God who was there in the founding of this country when our forefathers came here seeking the liberty to be able to seek God himself." At that time four guards came into the room and picked up the man and forced him out the door as he yelled, "You generation of vipers! I should have the right..." The doors were slam shut and the voice was heard no more.

The rest of the people stood quietly in their lines. Many were in shock, others laughed. But they all moved slowly towards their destiny. They all moved slowly into a "New World Order".

CHAPTER TWO

A Dark Day In France

Three years earlier in a sunny Fall Saturday morning, Deborah woke-up as she normally does on the weekend. She admired the sun's rays coming through the windows and across the bedroom as she grabbed the remote control to turn on the plasma TV on the wall. She could smell the coffee and she knew that her husband, Michael, will be coming through the bedroom door very soon with two fresh cups of coffee. This was their Saturday morning routine for seven years; she thought and smiled as she searched for the news. She couldn't help wonder where had the time flown. It was not perfect and they had many challenges, but they had the security of being with the right person, the peace that could only be experienced with love.

As the news caught Deborah's attention, Michael was arriving with the coffee.

"Good morning," Michael said as he handed the hot cup of coffee to Deborah.

"Good morning," Deborah whispered absent-minded.

Michael saw that Deborah was seized by the news. He turned to look at the screen and he couldn't believe his eyes. There was a city with homes on fire, lots of smoke, and people running around. Other people lay on the floor not moving. Now they both sat in silence listening to the reporter on the screen.

The reporter held the microphone and as he looked into the camera he spoke to the watching audience holding back his emotions as he stood surrounded by the carnage and the blood that covered the streets.

"I am standing in the "Quartier Latin" or the Latin Quarter of France in their main street, Boulevard St Michaell surrounded by destruction and death." The reporter spoke as you heard the sirens of the French Police, ambulance and firefighters in the background. "As far as we can tell, a car stopped close to the statue of Saint Michael slaying the "great dragon", Satan, which is in the middle of this congested area, blew up with tremendous impact. It seems that the driver perished with the car and everything seems to indicate that he was on a suicidal mission. This explosion occurred in the middle of the day, when the area is full of students from the 800 year old University, La Sorbonne and also with many tourists. There is rubble and glass everywhere. There are dead bodies as well as many injured people. Many people are helping others that are injured or are disoriented. It is impossible to know the amount of casualties at this moment. To make matters worse, my colleagues have informed me that two other sights have experience car explosions in France. One is St. Armand Circle and the other Rue de Passy. Both congested with tourists and many French people; both with many areas to shop and places to eat and visit.

This is a dark day for France. It takes us back to 2015, when France experienced a similar form of attack. No group has yet claimed the monstrosity committed here today. But it definitely seems like the work of a carefully planned act of terrorism. We will keep you updated with any information about this devastation."

As the reporter signed off the cameras moved slowly showing the area. People lay on the floor among the rubble, bathed in blood and not moving. Others walked as if in shock, not sure where to go. Some people were helping others to sit up; some were helping others to stand. Paramedics were trying to put some people in ambulances, while others were getting bandaged right there on the streets. There was dust from the exploding stores and cafes everywhere. There were bricks and glass all over the streets and cars. Firefighters were in different locations trying to desperately shut off the fires before they would cause other explosions; as firefighters and French officers try to bring people out of the partially standing buildings. There were children as well adults sitting on the sidewalks crying and hugging one another, comforting each other. A beat up baby carriage sat on its side on the sidewalk, surrounded by dust and bricks, as a yellow baby's blanket and a little teddy bear lay on the rubble. People were everywhere helping other people. Deborah and Michael watched the best of humanity come alive, in the result of the worst of human acts. Deborah's eyes were red, as a tear effortlessly escaped her eyes and ran down her cheek. Michael lowered his head and silently prayed. They both sat together absent-minded, as their coffees got cold.

CHAPTER THREE

The Eagle, The Sun And The Red Flag

It was before dawn and George Siegel was up and looking out the window of his New York penthouse with his first cup of coffee in his hand. It was 4 am Monday in New York, which meant it was 5 pm in China. It was time to start the game. He had his phone in his hand talking to his contact at the Shanghai Stock Exchange. George never slept much, three to four hours and the rest of the day was business. By the age of twenty-five he had made his first million and has spent the rest of his time making money off his money; turning his first million into billions. He was smart, ruthless and there was only one thing he loved more than money and that was the "game" of making money. But Siegel did not like to lose. He would buy, make his money and sale quickly as soon as he felt the stock reached its limit. He played with no conscience. Daewon had been his contact in China for a long time and they have a strong business phone relationship. One day Siegel asked Daewon what his name meant and Daewon answered, "Gracious God". Siegel informed Daewon that he had no use for God, but that he expected Daewon to commit some miracles and make some millions multiply.

"Daewon, what happened?" Siegel asked on the phone.

"The sun is not shining in the East, Siegel." Daewon answered.

"The hell with poetry shit, Daewon. What happened?"

"China's Shanghai Market is crashing. For the last three days in a row our three main stocks do not go up. NIKO dropped 15 points. Crude Oil is still dropping, this time 15 points and the one you wanted to test, NDC continued to go down 18 points. What do you want me to do?"

"Sell." Siegel said coldly.

"This will be devastating. You hold most of the shares in these companies. Selling will cause them to crash. Many people will lose their jobs."

"Sell. If your people are going to continue playing the game like children then they are going to squash themselves like roaches and they only have themselves to blame. I explained to you that this "Bubble" stock market game will not work. At first it will make these poor ignorant souls feel that they are making money, more money than they have seen all their lives. But it's a bubble and sooner or later bubbles burst and when they do the economy in China becomes very unstable. This is the "Major Leagues" and you don't put children to play with grown men. Sell."

"What do I do with the money?" Daewon asked.

"Nothing. Don't buy a thing. I want to see how this will affect New York."

"Talk to you later." Daewon said quickly. He knew that Siegel did not believe in idle talk.

"Yeah."

Siegel stood in his penthouse living room looking over New York. In the background the news was carrying on about France. Three hundred killed by a terrorist attack carried through by ISIS. He saw the film of ISIS celebrating and yelling "ALLAH". Siegel had a serious look in his face, as he whispered, "It's not going to be a good day."

By the end of the day, they were calling it "Black Monday". China had a domino effect, it scared people and the Dow Jones dropped 1,000 points. People were in fear all day long. The "Red Flag" was showing at 10:12 am when the drop was at 200 points. Afterward, it was total chaos; every hour worse than the one before as the drop continued.

Everyone was scared remembering "The Flash Crash" of 2010. When the S&P 500, DOW JONES Industrial Average and NASDAQ Composite collapsed and rebounded very rapidly. It dropped 998.5 points in a matter of 36 minutes. It was the 36 scariest minutes in the history of the New York Stock Exchange.

Today it was different. It was not a quick drop. It was a slow steady drop that mocked every stock broker and investor alike. Everyone was scared as they watched the numbers drop, everyone was waiting for the rebound and everyone was holding their breath watching the clock. When the bell rang at 4:00 pm S&P 500, Dow Jones and NASDAQ had dropped 1005 points. It was a devastating blow to the economy of the nation.

Siegel sat at night watching the news. He was very upset and he learned that it was best to be alone when he was angry. He sat in his robe, showered, his hair brushed back and holding a glass of bourbon in his hand. Today was an extra rough day; he had bourbon for breakfast, lunch and dinner. He sat quietly listening to the news.

The commentator went on, "Today, was "Black Monday" at Wall Street, where a devastating crash was experienced. It was a day of "Red Flags" since the drop began at 10:12 am. The Dow Jones, NASDAQ and S&P 500 dropped 1005 points. America's economy has been devastated. This was after China had intensively crashed dropping also 1,000 points. The competition for Crude Oil has become enormous in the globe since Iran has perfected its process and has become a competitor. Countries that need to buy oil do not care who they get the oil from, they just want it as cheap as possible. Because of this supply and demand competition the price of oil has dropped immensely. This is great news for the everyday consumers of gas, but devastating news for global economy."

"In related news," reporter continued, "Billionaire, John Stanza, committed suicide today. He was found in his office by his secretary with one shot to the head. His family was involved with oil. The family business went all the way back to his grandfather. We do not know how much money he loss. He leaves behind a wife, a son of 12 and a daughter of 10. Mr. Stanza was 49."

Siegel watched as he continued to drink his bourbon.

"Also," the commentator continued, "the Senior CEO of Wells Foods, John Wallace, whose products are sold in supermarkets across the nation, had a massive heart attack shortly after dealing with the news of his losses in the stock market. Mr. Wallace was 71 years old and had heart problems prior to this attack."

The reporter continued, "We are now transferring to the White House where the President is going to address the Nation."

The President was on the screen as he began to speak, "My fellow Americans, today we have received as a nation a very serious financial challenge. Our economy dropped at a very devastating level. I am here to tell you that our government is ready to work hard to turn this nation's economy around and bring us back to our feet. We must not panic. We must not get discouraged. Remember that our grandfathers lived through the "Great Depression" and the same way our country lifted itself up then, we will do so now. We will create new investments; we will create new jobs and a new dawn of opportunity will come for everyone in this country. Even though, our unemployment has reached at a level of 21%, because of unforeseen occurrences in companies throughout our nation that have been forced to close the doors of production; America has to stick together and I give you my word that we will bounce up and turn this economy around. Thank you and goodnight."

Siegel looked at the television with droopy eyes and disgusted. "Idiot," Siegel continued, "You didn't say a thing." His empty glass dropped to the floor as Siegel fell asleep.

The news continued showing a group of about 500 people standing in front of the White House protesting about the economy, the lack of jobs and the lack of answers from the President. They held signs up that read:

"THERE IS NO MIDDLE CLASS."

"TAXES ARE FOR THE WORKING CLASS."

"REFORM THE SYSTEM."

"FIRST: FAMILY, FOOD, FINANCES."

There were people holding up signs from New York, Texas, California and from all over the United States. A reporter walked up to one of the people leading the protest and asked, "What do you want to tell the viewers?"

An excited, intelligent young woman spoke up, "We are not here to start trouble. We have come from thousands of miles to make everyone aware, that the system does not work anymore. The President and the people running this country have to be aware that the gap between those who are rich and those who are trying to survive has become too big. The Middle Class has disappeared. We need jobs. We need lower taxes. We need affordable living and medical. We need a government reformation." People were yelling in support as the young lady spoke.

One calm gentleman dressed in a black turtleneck, black pants and a black raincoat stood quietly with a sign that read "IN GOD WE TRUST".

His calmness and sign caught the reporter's attention.

"Sir," she called out to him, "What is your name?"

"John," he answered with a calm voice.

"John, is there anything you like to tell our viewers?"

"Rome was very powerful in its days. But Rome turned away from God and the Roman Empire fell. This country was made of men who seek God. If we as a nation do not go back to respecting God; the Eagle will Fall."

The Reporter said, "Okay."

As the cameras focused on the people chanting; George Siegel continued his alcohol-induced sleep.

CHAPTER FOUR

The Secret Society

In a remote area of France, an old country home sat with great majesty alone in a wooded area, surrounded by an old black iron gate whose bars stood upright seven feet tall and topped with a perfectly spearhead point. The old house was made of stones and strong cedar wood, as it stood firmly and prestigiously for over five hundred years. The house had a cellar with many rooms and one of them was only for the finest wine collection found anywhere in Europe. It had two living levels with a total of sixteen rooms. Every room was grand and its decorations went back hundreds of years. Everywhere there was a gift, a memoir of someone important from France, Europe or the world. Rugs from leaders in the Middle East, original statues and paintings from Rome and Greece, decorations with jewels from India, ivory from Africa and antique artifacts found by archeologists in Egypt, Israel, South America and other parts of the world. Museums throughout the world have salivated over the fortune and the luxury of the historical items given to this aristocratic home, which has belonged for generations to a family which is part of a secret society unknown to the general population; but quite familiar to Presidents, Prime Ministers and billionaires from all over the world.

On this chilly clear night, as the full moon shined across the French sky, many expensive luxury cars were parked in front of the historical house; cars that belonged to world leaders; as well as billionaire business men. Tonight this secret "Dark Society" was holding a meeting like they have not held in a long time. Tonight it was not a meeting of "blood rituals" or "virgin sacrifices" after mortifying sexual gang rapes; tonight was an all "business" meeting which involved unknowingly to the general population, their future and destiny.

The fireplace was alive with dancing flames that glowed in the semi dark room, which added to the alluring mystic in the house. Every person in the room had on a black robe. The robe had a red thin line going down the sleeves and on top of the wide black hood, that covered the faces of the members, was an eye embroiled in white. Everyone knew everyone in the elite group of the secret society, but no one ever saw anyone's face in the congregations or assembly of the brotherhood of the illuminated Dark Society.

A gentleman of advanced years, whose voice shook as he spoke and his wrinkled hand with brown spots showed through the wide opening of the sleeves, got up to speak. No one dared to complain about his slow movements or speech for he had been part of the Dark Society since he was young man and now he was an elder whose power around the world was even unknown to the younger generations within the group. But it was known that many world leaders had lost their lives because they were not willing to listen to the much younger voice of this man back in the 50's and 60's.

"Brothers, we are gathered here tonight like our ancestors, like the beginning of time at the Tower of Babel."

The people in the room yelled in unison, "Here, Here!"

"We are the illuminated minds that have worked so hard throughout the ages to unite the world, creating a world government and bank, as well as a unified world religion; continuing the great work of those before us like Leonardo Da Vinci, Sir Isaac Newton, Sir Winston Churchill, Carl Marx and many more. How surprised would the world be to know of the list of people, whose ghostly footsteps we follow, in the creation of a united world government?"

The gentlemen in the room yelled, "Here, here, Brother!" agreeing with the words of the elder. Some of the men were listening quietly and would nod their heads in agreement.

"It is the ignorance of the masses," the elder continued, "and the hypocrisy of the religious piety that surrounds us that has fought our efforts throughout generations. But we are the chosen generation that will bring the desire and dreams of our forefathers to fruition. Finally, a New World Order will come to existence, my Brothers."

THE TIME HAS COME

Everyone in the room clapped in agreement and enthusiasm, as they felt motivated and regenerated by the wise words of the elder. The elder continued to welcome all the brothers and made a few ritual comments pertaining to the Dark Society creed. After finalizing his words the elder introduced the American billionaire, George Siegel. Siegel was only one of the twenty-five members that were here tonight, but he was important because his business was a bridge that linked Europe with the United States. Many like to say that Siegel had many powerful Americans in his hands, he use to correct them and say, "I have their balls and I could squeeze them all I want," and then Siegel would laugh. There were other billionaires from Hollywood, California all the way to the Middle East; it was a united nations of illuminated minds.

Siegel began to speak, "What occurred in the United States on Black Monday was a big sign. The United States is in a financial decadence. Since our Brother, a President of the United States during the 90's, whose name I have to respect, America has not seen a prosperous economy again and all the Senate does is talk about the National Deficit and raising taxes. While the middle class was happy in the United States, we were able to maintain the illusion of the American dream alive. But now the balance is disappearing in America. The middle class is disappearing. The government is running out of funds to maintain the masses fat and happy, and they are becoming wise to the fact that the country is being run by ten very rich and powerful billionaires that run the whole show. The Voting process is a joke and controlled by a few, the Judicial System is anything but legal for we know that 'We' the billionaires are basically untouchable and the rest of the government agencies are in upheaval and corrupt. Now all this was fine with people like us, except that once the middle class is not fat and happy, and there is a visible margin between "Us" and "Them", revolution will occur."

Siegel was quiet for a few minutes and one of the elders spoke up, "Brother, what do you suggest? Obviously, you have meditated on this matter. Do you bring a request to the table?"

Siegel cleared his throat, "Yes." He chose his words carefully. "First of all, I suggest to everyone that we do not keep our investments in American banks, but it would be safer to keep our investments in our accounts outside of the United States for now."

The brothers were surprised at this request and one of them spoke up, "This will be a very hard blow to the economy of the United States. We are talking about an amount of money whose number I cannot even foresee. It would be devastating to the American economy."

"This is something that we will have to meditate on and take every detail into consideration, Brother Siegel. We know you are an expert and that you are speaking for our greater good, but we also have, some very good investment in America. America is a money making machine. But we will meditate further on your observation."

"Thank you." Siegel returned.

"Was there something else, Brother Siegel?" The elder asked.

"Yes. We have spoken about this in the past. The President of the United States is no longer meeting our criteria. He has hurt our plans for the United States, for the spread of the Micro-Bio Chip implant, for the Trans-Atlantic of North America and Europe Commerce, for the involvement of the United States in the European Movement; he has gone against everything we have suggested to him and he does not budge."

"We have spoken about this before," one of the elders reminded Siegel.

"We did agree that if things did not change with the President of the United States, that we were going to be force to take action for the greater good." Another elder reminded everyone.

"I think the time has come," Siegel stated firmly.

"That is a very serious statement, Brother Siegel. You think we have reached the point of having to assassinate the President of the United States?"

"Yes, and the Vice-President understands our goals," Siegel stated.

"Yes, definitely the Vice-President has shown his allegiance to our cause." The Elder agreed.

"Well, we have been considering this for a while, now. Thank you, Brother Siegel. Anything else?" The elder asked.

"No, thank you." Siegel sat down.

THE TIME HAS COME

Then without a word the crimson colored curtains opened. A tall figure with a black robe, that had gold lines going down the shoulders and sleeves and on the hood he had an embroiled eye in gold. The room was silent as he stood there quietly. A minute passed, five minutes passed and the room was in total silence. It did not matter how much money any of these guys had or how powerful they thought they were. This figure in front of them was the head of the Dark Society and many dark societies around the world, including some of the most prestigious universities throughout the world. The masses live surrounded by a smoke screen that blinds them from seeing the reality of who controls the world. They work so hard to survive and to make their dreams come true, not realizing that their world is run by a very small group of people whose money, legacy and power controls everything and this man manipulates and leads every man in this room.

"All of you have been summoned here tonight and are part of an elite group. You have been chosen and are truly blessed to be part of a lineage that goes back to "The Tower of Babel". Do not fail me. For you know who I am. I am, the One that was to come and unite the world in one government, one bank and one religion. It is very important that the European Nations come together. Europe will be our door to a World Government. At this point we have to deal with Prime Minister Taylor of England. But I assure you that every move I make is precise and very soon it will lead to one goal. Bosnia seems out of control to the world; but Bosnia is our link between the Middle East and Europe. We will not allow Bosnia to be in the forefront of the New European Union like in the past. But we will not treat Bosnia disrespectfully. I know how Bosnia is playing an important part in the New World Government.

We are parts of a big puzzle unimaginable to the masses in the globe. But every piece is carefully designed by our illuminated minds; Goodnight, gentlemen." At that point the shadowy figure disappeared behind the curtains.

Everyone held tight to every word. The meeting of the "Dark Society" continued among the other members through the night. No one mentioned the shadowy figure again, but everyone heard his words and they all knew that the times were changing.

CHAPTER FIVE

One World Government

The Prime Minister of England walked calmly down the halls of the Palace of Westminster. He wore a dark navy suite without a wrinkle, a starched crisp white long sleeve shirt and a scarlet tie with dark blue thin lines. His black shoes were perfectly shined. His face was thin, but strong. His body was without an ounce of fat and toned. He was known for his strong mind, sharp tongue and his calm disposition. His eyes were deep blue and many felt calmed by his look, others felt pierced by his eyes. It depended on whether he was content or displeased with the person. But mostly everyone agreed that Prime Minister Damian Taylor was the most charismatic Prime Minister that England had ever seen.

He always had two "bodyguards" with him. But these two gentlemen were actually at his disposition and they knew him better than anyone. They reached the doors of the meeting room where other European leaders waited, but the doors were not opened. The bodyguards always waited for the signal and Prime Minister Damian Taylor always loved to make people wait, especially dignitaries, Presidents and other Prime Ministers. He had all the patience in the world and he loved playing mind games.

He walked into the room and very politely excused himself as he welcomed every single person. Both bodyguards stayed outside. Shaking their hands and looking at their eyes. Always smiling and saying something a little personal to each. "How are the children?" "Say hello to your wife for me." "I hope your father is doing better." He knew everyone's weakness. Everyone admired him. He gave a special hug of reassurance to the President of France, President Timeo Dubois. He then looked around the room as he smiled to the group of leaders. On one side of the table there was the President of Portugal and the

Prime minister of Spain. At the other side there was the President of Germany and the President of Poland. Strategically, he made sure that the "greeters" had the President of France at the end of the table, parallel to where he sat in front of everyone.

Prime Minister Taylor began the meeting. "Welcome my friend. I feel obligated to welcome, President Dubois and to let you know that we are ready to help you in any way we can."

"Thank you, my friend. The United Nations and the United States have been trying to help us very candidly."

The Prime Minister Taylor smiled, "Yes, I am sure they have. Unfortunately, the U.S. has major problems of their own with the occurrence of "Black Monday" and the fact that they are thousands of miles away; they could never quite understand the European way of life. The United Nations has become extremely "political" and personally I am not too happy with their way of thinking in the last few years. The old European Union was not united enough and our union has done very little for our safety against terrorism. Bosnia and Herzegovina have become more of a liability than strength to our union. Their youth are leaving their country to join Middle East radical groups and become terrorists. They have easy access to our nations because they are Europeans and this has become a problem. We must change our ways of dealing with these mortal pestilence."

Everyone started to talk at the same time. The Prime Minister of Spain spoke the loudest and took over the floor. He was a short, square head, square shoulder, strong man that people refer to as the "Bulldog". He was very stubborn and spoke loud scratchy voice. "I have hoped for a truly united Europe for a long time, since the beginning of the Euro. We need to strengthen the Euro."

Prime Minister Taylor looked at him and answered, "Yes, that's what I expected you to say." Prime Minister Taylor knows that all "Bulldog" cared about was money.

"Now, please gentleman wait a minute," the President of Germany interrupted. He was a very analytical thin man. Very light skin, which always looked sickly but never, was. He was very intelligent and it was one of the few people in the room that Prime Minister Taylor liked. He really didn't care if the rest of them burned in hell. But President Fischer was more practical and cold. He wanted to understand what Prime Minister Taylor was exactly saying.

"Exactly, what do you mean when you say that Europe needs to unite? Are we talking strictly finances or what else? Also, is keeping Bosnia and Herzegovina out of the New European Union a smart move? The fact is that I agree with you, they are a liability. Bosnia is a time bomb, but wouldn't it be better to keep them close and keep an eye on them?" President Fischer asked coldly.

Prime Minister Taylor stood quietly in front of the group and waited as he looked at them, like a snake, and he chose his words carefully. He knew he captivated their attention. Now the true "game of chess" began. If he could convince at least two of the five, his job would become a lot easier; definitely, less bloodshed. Three of the five would be a gift and a surprise. Convincing all five was not expected and it wouldn't be much fun. After all, the game of "words" was no comparison to the game of "action". "Action" was more fun.

"The world has been constantly changing since after World War II. The Middle East has slowly become more powerful and dangerous. What has happened to France can and will happen very easily to anyone of us. It's only a matter of time. The US and the UN move too slowly. ISIS and other radical Middle East groups have infiltrated our countries. Our hearts want to help their refugees. I feel for those people. But my mind fears them, because we don't know if it's a refugee escaping or a terrorist attacking. Bosnia cannot control its people, so how can we think that they can do anything for Europe. We cannot continue to carry them. I agree, we have to keep an eye on them, but we cannot allow the 'ticking bomb' to explode in our faces." Prime Minister Taylor spoke very strongly.

"What do you propose that we do?" Asked President Dubois.

"We create a conglomerate." Prime Minister Taylor spoke slowly as he studied each reaction. "We create a 'World Government' in Europe."

Prime Minister Taylor stopped talking. It was time for him to be silent and watch the reactions.

As Prime Minister Taylor expected the President of Spain broke the silence, "I thought we were here to talk about the economy and how to make the Euro more powerful. I don't want to talk about any World Government. Is that what you meant when you told me you had an idea to unite Europe even more and to make it more powerful?" The Bull was showing.

"I like the idea. It definitely sounds interesting." Said President Dubois.

The President of Poland broke in, "It would be too much of a reformation of government. It seems like an insane idea. I am not even sure how the UN would see this movement."

Prime Minister Taylor smiled at Dubois, "I knew you would like it."

"Gentlemen," Dubois continued, "we must agree that Europe has been through hell: first, with Hitler and World War II, now the shadows of the Middle East with their refugees and ISIS. These people are fanatics. There is no reasoning with them. How many times must one of our countries experience death and destruction before we come together? Even the United States have their 9/11. They can get attacked again at any time like we did in France. These people have infiltrated our countries. We live with the enemy. It's a different type of war than World War II. These people move like shadows. We need to unite. We don't have to lose the identity of our own country. We just have to unite and help one another."

"Of course we don't have to lose our identity." Prime Minister Taylor continued, "France will be French and Germany will be German but we can create laws, agreements and share weapons and man power to help each other stay safe. We can protect one another from terrorism; instead of continuing idle conversations in European meetings where we complain and talk but we take no action to create a safe Europe, we can unite to prepare concretely against terrorism."

"I am not in." The Prime Minister Spain spoke emphatically.

The President of Germany smiled slightly and asked, "World government and protection?"

Prime Minister Taylor nodded.

"It almost sounds as if you are trying to take over the world without going to war. Thank God we all know each other very well."

Everyone laughed.

Prime Minister Taylor smiled and spoke, "We will all finally have peace." Then turning to the Prime Minister of Spain he continued. "Then we can work together to make our dream come true. We can work together to make the Euro more powerful than the American dollar."

The Prime Minister of Spain was quiet.

The President of Poland spoke and agreed strongly with the Prime Minister of Spain.

"I don't like the sound of a World Government. I like the idea of all helping one another against terrorism. But we need more information as to how you propose that this World Government will work respecting the individual laws of each nation. How will the World Government be run and what are its ideals? Right now, with this much information, I have to say no."

"Everyone here will receive a written form of the ideas behind the World Government. I ask you to please read it and dissect it. I welcome you to give me feedback. We can all work together for a better Europe. I know I can count with France and Germany."

They both nodded.

The President of Poland stated, "I will read it, but I am not interested in a World Government. I also would like to feel better with how we deal with Bosnia and Herzegovina."

Then the President of Portugal broke his silence, "I will read it and definitely I like the idea to unify Europe and protect each other. I will give you my opinion and feedback. But we do have to sale the idea to our people. Will our people accept this union of a World Government?"

Prime Minister Damian Taylor smiled and answered, "People all want the same thing, to feel safe and to have a prosperous life for their children. The World Government will provide for the people of Europe what they want...peace and prosperity." As he said this he thought to himself, I definitely have France and Germany, checkmate.

CHAPTER SIX

One Faith, One Spirit, One Word

Pastor Joaquin Silva was a short man with dark skin, curly jet black hair with a dab of gray around the side burns and deep dark brown eyes. He stood at five- feet and four inches, with a small skinny frame. He always stood very straight like a military man and he always kept himself very clean and groomed. He was a very educated man. He had degrees in Psychology and Theology. Portuguese was his language of origin but he also spoke Spanish, French, and English. He spoke very proper English but with a heavy Brazilian accent. His knowledge of the "Word of God" made him stand-out in any room or church. His faith in "Jesus" was full of passion since the first day he accepted Jesus in his life. He spoke with knowledge, love and a conviction that made others listen. He was a man of God. His congregation struggled; getting the bills paid and keeping his little church, Global Baptist Church of God, opened was a challenge. Being a pastor, a husband and a father to two teenage boys was overbearing, but he never showed the stress. He was always very firm in his faith.

About a month after the attack in France, Michael and Deborah joined Pastor Silva and some people from the congregation at the church. It was a special meeting requested by Pastor Silva and only certain people from the congregation were present as the rain fell hard and steady outside. Everyone that Pastor Silva called was faithfully present. Michael and Deborah have known Pastor Silva for three years and have always felt comfortable in his presence. After they joined his congregation they never looked elsewhere to worship God. The other couple was Antonio and Isadora; they were both in their early sixties. Both knew Pastor Silva from Brazil and continued with him in the States. There was a tall man by the name of Yannel Schul. He had black curly hair and beard. His eyes were dark and very observant. He spoke English with a very heavy Yiddish accent. He was born in Israel and as an adult he converted from his Jewish faith to Christianity. He loved and missed his family and old friends at his Jewish Temple in New York. One day to his own amazement he was "touched" by Jesus, as he describes it and his life changed forever. Yannel went through a very painful struggle, almost metaphysical, and the life he knew since childhood ended. As time went by and he grew in his Christian faith he has experience a freedom and joy that he had never experienced before. But he knows that even though he is a Christian by faith, he will always be an Israelite by birth and he will always love his land and his people.

There was one person at the meeting, even though he was the newest member of the congregation; Pastor Silva had great respect for him. The tall slender man had an incredible knowledge of the "Word of God". His prayers were filled with love and peace. His messages touched the hearts of those who listened. When you spoke to him, he would listen with his heart, soul and mind. When he spoke to you, his words would alleviate your inner pain with serenity. He always wore his black raincoat with a black turtleneck. Even though no one knew him fully, everyone felt very comfortable to be in the same room with him. His presence radiated peace. He was embraced by the congregation very quickly and they all knew him simply as John. His knowledge of languages was very versatile. He was heard speaking in English, Spanish, Portuguese, French and God only knows what other languages he mastered, because he never spoke of himself. John did everything peacefully and he never was in a hurry.

The Pastor started the meeting after a small prayer from Isadora.

"My brothers and sisters," the Pastor started saying, "I want to thank you all for coming here tonight in such short notice and in the rain. Unfortunately, there are some major things happening around the world that are very important and will affect our lives as Christians. Other Pastors will also be having similar meetings with their congregation. I want to have a meeting with the rest of our congregation, but I chose first to meet with you guys alone. It is very important that our congregation prays together and also help one another to stand firm in our faith. There are many changes happening in our world and we need to understand how we stand "biblically" versus the popular opinions of the population. I feel that very difficult times are heading our way and our faith will be tested beyond our imagination."

"You mean like what happened with France?" Deborah asked.

"What happened in France is a result of the situation." Pastor Silva continued, "We have ISIS in the Middle East and countries like Iraq and Iran who will continue their practice of a faith which includes a strong hate towards the west. A week ago one-hundred thirty-one Christians were killed in Jerusalem and it was not even reported by the media or covered by the news because it was kept perfectly quiet."

"Meu Deus!" Isadora exclaimed.

"If it's true, why would they keep it quiet? These terrorist like to promote their actions?" Michael asked.

"When it comes to Christians, it's different." Pastor Silva explained. "They hate the Christians and they want to keep the Christian persecutions as quiet as possible, so that we feel safe and our guards are down."

"Thank God this is not happening in America." Antonio stated.

"Not yet." John said.

"You believe that there will be a Christian persecution in the US?" Yanel asked.

"Definitely," John answered.

"I am sorry but I find that very hard to believe. This country would have to change so much." Yanel stated very emphatically.

"I am sorry but I have to agree with Yanel. I find it very difficult to believe that there would be a Christian persecution in the United States." Michael added.

"The crash at Wall Street and the financial instability of this nation is going to create a lot of fear and changes in this country that will cause a great division." John said.

"Pastor, if this Christian persecution in Jerusalem was kept so quiet; how do you know about it?" Deborah asked.

"I only know about it because of my connections with my Christian brothers and friends in Jerusalem. Remember I lived there for three years before coming to the US. I received a phone call the day after the killings. I actually lost one of my best friends." The Pastor said as his voice cracked a little and his eyes watered. He cleared his throat and moved on. "The strange thing about the massacre is that ISIS did not claim the act. It was another group in the Middle East. In the meantime ISIS and these groups are moving more and more towards Europe and I feel that Europe will unite to retaliate against ISIS and others in the Middle East. The eruption will be very bloody."

"You make it sound so definite." Michael stated.

"Well I said that there will be major changes in this country that we must prepare for; one of them is the Biochip implants. The United States is seriously considering of investing millions of dollars making sure that everyone gets a biochip placed in their hand in the name of "technological progress". The country is in debt. People are without jobs. People are either rich or trying to survive and the government is concern with the implant of Biochips. It's not right. Everyone is free to do as they wish. God gave us free will. But let me be clear that as Christians we must refuse implanting the Biochip in the temple of God; our bodies."

"What do you think is the meaning of all these things happening?" Antonio asked.

The strong, peaceful voice carried across the room, "The time has come." John never said much but when he spoke he was felt. Everyone looked his way.

Yannel squint his intelligent eyes, as his face wrinkled and repeated the phrase in the form of a question, "The time has come?"

"The 'time' for what?" Michael asked.

"It is time for those things written in the book of 'Revelations' to come to past."

"So it's the end of time," Antonio said mockingly, "the end of the world."

"Not the end of the world." John spoke calmly, "The end of the world as we know it, and the beginning of sorrows to come. The end is not yet. It is a time for wars, famine, and pestilence; the beginning of sorrows." John spoke these words as he looked into Pastor Silva's eyes.

"Our brother John is correct, my brothers. The more we study 'The Book of Daniel' and 'Revelations' the better we can understand what is happening. We believe that the Anti-Christ is here. He has not made himself known, but we believe that he is slowly bringing his plan to fruition."

Isadora exclaimed, "Meu, Deus!"

Deborah asked, "The Anti-Christ? Revelations is happening now? God forbid."

"We cannot be sure who the Anti-Christ is right now. He has not made himself known, yet." Pastor Silva continued, "But the Bible teaches us to learn to read the signs and we see the signs all around us. Since Israel became a country in 1945 until now; every decade that passes, the signs have become stronger. I believe the Anti-Christ has arrived and that he is somewhere in the Middle East or Europe or God knows where. But where ever he is, he is preparing to carry out his plans."

"So, what do we do?" Michael asked.

"We Christians have to stick together. We must pray and prepare. Our faith has to be more united than ever. It is no longer about denominations. It's about one Faith; one Spirit; one Word. Pastors from our area are preparing a meeting in a few weeks so that Christian churches all over come together in one place to pray, to be informed and to plan."

Michael said softly but loud enough to be heard, "I can't believe this is true."

Then Antonio asked in his heavy Brazilian accent, "What about this, how do you say, chip?"

Michael answered Antonio, "The Biochip is a small (micro) computer chip, inserted under the skin, for identification purposes. As time goes by, the chip will be the key to do many things in society. Life as we know it today will cease to exist."

"What do you mean when you say, 'the key'?" Isadora asked.

Michael continued, "The Chip will be the top form of identification. It will be used as a passport when you travel. People would be able to use it to pay for whatever they buy because it would be connected to their bank accounts. Your medical history will be there. You will be able to turn your car on with it and open the doors to your car and home. The list is almost infinite of the numerous things a person will be able to do with the Micro Chip. Also works as a GPS and Children will never get lost."

Antonio continued comically, "So the wife will always know where I am."

Everyone laughed as Antonio said, "Caralho," a bad word in Portuguese.

Isadora pinched him, Antonio apologized to the Pastor.

The Pastor smiled, "Antonio Isadora has a human GPS already on you."

"That's right," Isadora continued, "it's my heart. My heart tells me he did something wrong and then, I pinch him."

Everyone laughed.

"Pastor Silva, do you feel this 'Chip' in the hand is what Revelation refers to when it speaks about the 'Number of the Beast'?" Yannel asked.

The Pastor thought very carefully about his answer, as Deborah's cell phone sounded a message.

The Pastor said, "Yes, I believe it."

Yannel continued, "But if the Chip is as important as Michael said and you are saying that Christians are not to get the Chip, then what are we supposed to do? How do we survive?"

"We must stick together like true brothers and sisters in Christ and help one another."

The room was silent as everyone pondered on the Pastor's answer. The silence was broken by Deborah, "My God!"

"What's wrong?" Michael asked.

"On my phone I just got a message. There has been a terrorist attack in Spain, in the city of Madrid. They believe it was a civil movement against the government. I don't know how many died; but it was very bloody."

The group sat quietly and John began to pray. His voice embracing the hearts of all present.

CHAPTER SEVEN

The Reign In Spain

The Summer rain covered the city of Madrid. It was right before dawn, still dark and the Prime Minister of Spain sat in his home office in the "Palacio de la Moncloa". Alejandro Rojas de Sevillas was a short, strong man that was known as the "Bulldog". He was five feet one inch tall and built like a cinderblock. The "Bulldog" was very intelligent and trusted his instincts; his weakness was his stubbornness. His favorite moment of the day was early in the morning when he could sit with his "Café Negro" and his thoughts. These days he had many thoughts.

He had two phones in his home office, one had five lines that everyone had access to, if they were family, friends or intelligent enough to do everything in their power to find the phone number of the "Prime Minister" of Spain. The other phone had one line and it was a very private number that only a very carefully selected group of people throughout the planet had. This early morning in the middle of "Café Negro", silence and the rain the second phone was ringing. "The Bulldog" looked at it intrigued and at the same time with indifference, as it rang once, twice, three times. After the third ring he said, "Hello", with a heavy scratchy voice.

"Hello, my friend," said the soft friendly voice on the line. A voice that you could tell was smiling, even though, you can't see the face. The "Bulldog" knew who he was and truly did not wish to speak to him.

"Mierda!" he said in his rough voice.

"Ouch! I do have feelings." The voice continued to smile.

"Prime Minister Taylor, I don't mean any disrespect, but if you call this early in this line, there better be a good reason."

The Prime Minister of England continued, "Yes, of course. I know you are sitting in your office with your "Café Negro" in silence, contemplating on your next moves. I respect and understand the importance of solitude and the importance of dissecting and digesting ones thoughts. But that is why I called," the "Bulldog" listened intently with a wrinkled forehead, "so that you and I could speak to each other as two civilized, intelligent leaders without interruptions."

Prime Minister Taylor stopped. There was silence. No response from the "Bulldog"; he was hard.

"The other day at the meeting," continued Prime Minister Taylor, "I think, you and I, unfortunately, ended the meeting in a disagreement. Intelligent minds will always disagree because the nature of thought will always create different views; an argument. That's why I respect you, because you think. You are not a puppet. Now, obviously, we both want the best for Europe. I respect you enough to want to sort out our differences."

"The Bulldog" listened and like always, waited to collect his thoughts and then spoke sincerely, "Prime Minister Taylor, I have listened to you and now I need you to listen to me." The "Bulldog" spoke English with a very heavy Spanish accent; but clearly, "I disagree, that you and I ended the meeting with a disagreement or a problem. Our "problem" was already there before the meeting started. I do not trust you. If it's true that you are as respectful and educated as you claim to be, then you would respect my request to be left out of this "European" or "Global" union that you are seeking. The "Euro" is business. Business is business and I am all for that; but this "One World Government" seems more like a quiet "totalitarian" movement to try to control a group of nations without going to war. Let me be frank, I don't trust you."

The Prime Minister continued very calmly, "I am not trying to dictate what to do. If I came across strongly, I apologize. I mentioned to everyone present that I wrote a proposal laying out the ideas and that I would respect any feedback for improving the changes. We are talking about the safety of Europe and coming together to do away with terrorism."

"Terrorism? I have this country at a level 4 and we are much secured. I am confident that we are doing everything possible to keep our people safe from terrorism."

There was silence. Prime Minister Taylor continued, "Now I understand. Your problem is not stubbornness. Your problem is that you truly feel safe. You honestly believe that no act of terrorism can be committed in Spain. Do you remember March of 2004? Let me refresh your memory with some numbers: ten bombs, three trains, 191 people killed, 1,800 people injured, why would you feel safe?"

"You don't need to remind me of the history of Spain. Think what you like. Say what you wish. But do me a favor. No, not a "favor"; I demand that you listen and respect my "Instruction" to you, do not call me back. As the "Bulldog" completed his sentence he hung-up the phone. The Prime Minister of England sat with the receiver in his hand listening to the dial tone in the dark as he said, "Pride goes before destruction. Proverb 16:18... my friend."

It was a beautiful clear night in Madrid, Spain. The soft summer Iberia breeze was in the air as the sky was lit by a beautiful fool moon and a myriad of stars shined like diamonds. It was the perfect night, as the citizens of Spain, as well as tourists, consumed the streets to feast. All over, there were people in the streets eating, drinking and shopping. It was a perfect peaceful night; that seemed far away from the harsh realities of life and the world. The night life at "La Gran Via" in Madrid was flourishing. "La Gran Via" is a very long street that runs from "Plaza de Espana" to the "Plaza de los Cibeles" and along the way it is lit with lights from cafes, restaurants, expensive shops, theaters, and night clubs. There were lights and people everywhere. It is known as the "Rodeo Drive" of Spain. Some people were eating indoors and many others outdoors. People were drinking and dancing as they hopped from club to club. Love was everywhere as people held hands and others kissed openly. It was miles of "amor y fiesta" in the summer breeze of Spain.

As the feast continued in "La Gran Via" a Volvo with only a driver pulled in front of the "Palacio de la Moncloa". The gates to the residency were closed. The place was lit and the Prime Minister Rojas was having a quiet moment with his wife and a couple close to them. They conversed peacefully as they drank "Felipe Segundo" after dinner. One of the guards watched the Volvo pull over and stop. As one guard stayed by the gate the other one walked to the car. The car exploded killing the driver and the two guards. The explosion was loud and the impact shattered the windows in the front of the house. The glass flew into the house and spread throughout the dining area where the Prime Minister, his wife and his guests ate. Glass flew into the face of the Prime Minister's wife and into the backside of their guest. Both were on the floor screaming in pain. The Prime Minister ran to his wife and held her under the table and the visitor's wife held her husband also under the table. They didn't know if the attack was over. Everyone was shaking, as the ladies yelled uncontrollably and blood was all over them. Everything happened in a matter of seconds.

Three guards in the house came running into the room and in a matter of seconds they had radioed for help and they moved everyone to the corner of the next room. In a matter of five minutes five police cars, two fire trucks, two ambulances and the Bomb Squat were all at the "Palacio de la Moncloa". Everyone concerned for the safety of the Prime Minister and his wife. As the feast continued down "La Gran Via" people were unaware of the commotion at the "Palacio de la Moncloa". They continued to enjoy their jubilee. But every officer was all over the Prime Minister's house.

Ten men carrying automatic weapons "SP901's" covered with paper bags, situated themselves blocks away from each other all along the "La Gran Via". These men all were dressed in black with black hats and a thin black scarf around their necks. Their faces were not covered, but in a chaotic moment, it would be difficult to identify them with the hats and scarf. Their watches were synchronized and ten minutes after the explosion at the Prime Minister's residence, while everyone party on the streets dancing, eating and drinking in this beautiful perfect night, they began to shoot freely into the crowds with their automatic weapons. All alone different spots of "La Gran Via" innocent feasting people were getting shot and killed, as bullets flew shattering glass windows of stores and restaurants. People on the streets were falling dead, as others ran and others tripped and were trampled. People sitting at restaurants and cafes outside were being killed. Blood and chaos were everywhere at different areas of "La Gran Via". People were screaming and running for safety, but not knowing where it was all coming from.

The few scattered police officers that stayed behind were confused and as they drew their guns out they were careful not to shoot innocent people. One officer was close to one of the shooters and was able to kill him. The whole attack lasted for no more than five minutes. Then as quickly as these men appeared, they disappeared. As they ran they yelled, "El govierno del pueblo! Abajo con el Bulldog!" Which was Spanish for, "The people's government! Down with the Bulldog!" As the men disappeared they left behind a massacre of dead and injured bodies. Bodies, blood and glass covered "La Gran Via" from "La Plaza de Espana" to the "Plaza de los Cibeles".

As the smoke cleared and the news got back to Prime Minister Rojas, he was told that the men doing the shooting were heard yelling as they ran, "Govierno del pueblo!" and "Abajo con el Bulldog!"

One of his chief advisors spoke into his ear, "Sir; I think this was a civil movement against the government. The shooters were from Spain."

Prime Minister Roja's face was red with anger.

"No one was captured?" he asked.

"Only one of their men was killed. He is a citizen of Spain and a Muslim."

Prime Minister Roja realized that the car explosion in front of his house was a decoy. Both attacks were connected and they never meant to kill him. If this was a true revolt against him, then he would have been assassinated. He sat in his chair pondering the situation.

CHAPTER EIGHT

Divided We Fall

The President of the United States sat with his Chief Advisor having a private conversation as they shared a cup of coffee in the Oval Office. They both have known each other for a many years and the Chief Advisor Karl Garrett was a genius political mind. He was in his early forties, medium built, with brown hair and brown beard. Karl was passionate about his job, power and he has made an art out of manipulating minds without getting caught. The President had two other advisors which were part of the "Incumbent" group of advisors that the President listens to in his most distressed moments. Karl did not care for them. He saw them as insects pestering his garden of power; even though, he smiled and played the political game. In actuality, he wished to dissipate them out of his presence when he sat with the "Commander in Chief".

"Sir," Karl spoke with precision and very intense, "the crash on Wall Street has devastated the economy. It is not budging and I do not see the economy going up any time soon. People are losing their faith in us because the unemployment is at 30% and there are no signs of jobs. People with money do not want to invest because of the instability of the economy and the middle class is basically disappearing. We cannot allow a big gap between the poor and the rich to be obvious or we will have a strong revolt in our society. We need to create jobs and keep our nation fat and happy."

The President listened attentively and spoke very softly, almost a whisper, "Fat and happy. As long as everything 'seems' fine and people go about their business enjoying their personal 'American Dream', they stay fat and happy."

"That's America, Sir." Karl said emphatically.

"Have we really become such an empty, self-serving, nation?" The President asked.

"No. Once in a while we get a historical hero that comes in the name of change or love and they bring together a group and make it seem like we are more united as a nation and sometimes they even go as far as creating changes, for what? So, that when the storm passes our citizens go back to their personal dreams and continue to live in their alienated self-serving lives. That's America, Sir."

"What do you propose that we do, Karl?"

"We have to go back to basics in this country. We have to go back to manufacturing."

"Most companies want to take the manufacturing out of the country because it's cheaper. How are we supposed to change that to help our economy?" The President asked.

"We have an incredible amount of illegal immigrants in this country that are willing to do whatever it takes to stay here. We make a deal with the manufacturing companies to bring their manufacturing back to America at an extremely low tax. They are going to make money and we are going to make more money, too. We create an Immigration work plan, where we allow these illegal immigrants to become legal aliens, as long as they work for the manufacturing companies and we tax the hell out of them. If they quit they will be deported. The corporations are happy making money with low taxes; we still get a substantial amount, more than if they continue to manufacture outside. In the meantime, we tax the hell out of the workers, they will be happy because they will be living the American dream legally. Any problems or complaints, we sent their asses back to where they came from."

"Do you think this can work? I know it's unethical but desperate times, call for desperate measures. Correct?" The President asked.

"Correct. Now listen to me, we also have to implement the Biochip." Karl continued.

The President looked at him with an inquisitive look. "With the Biochip we will be able to track these new "legal aliens" and make sure that they keep up to their part of the bargain. If they don't, we find them and deport them. They can't run away."

"Do we do the Biochip for everyone or only the new legal aliens?" President asked.

"Everyone; we are going to have a control over this nation like never before. We have to unite with Prime Minister Taylor and his work with the unification of Europe and keep this nation afloat before it crashes and we find ourselves in a depression deeper than any we have ever experienced. If we play the game right, no one has to know that all we are doing is saving our asses." Karl looked at the President with intensity in his eyes.

The President nodded. "We have to create a 'Special Work Program' to legalize these people. We have to create a proposal and figure out how to pass it through the senate," said the President.

"I have this. I will put the proposal together. I will take care of the Senate. I will pull the strings and call every favor owed to me."

"Karl," the President got his attention, "do we share this with Frank and Jenna?" These were the other two advisors.

Karl gave the President a look of indifference, as he replied, "The less people know; the better for the country."

Pastor Joaquin Silva was at his church, Global Baptist Church of God in Buffalo, Upstate New York with his congregation. There were about twenty-five people this Sunday morning. It was a good turnover and it made him feel like his work for God was being fruitful. He looked around and he remembered the days that he sat in his small church with his wife, his two sons and his old friends Antonio and Isadora. They would read the "Word" of God, sing praises and pray to God. Then he would stand in front of them and give a message with the same amount of passion as if he had a full church. Pastor Silva always said, "That Praise and prayer is what we give to God; but the message is what God gives to us." He always thought it was a shame that some people do not listen to the message, with the same energy that they pray or sing praises to God.

Today was a beautiful day, the lights were dim, and the speakers were playing a soft Portuguese gospel song "Deus de Promesas". People were standing with their eyes closed, some had their hands up, some cried while others smiled, some seemed as if in a trance. Everyone believed that they felt the energy of the Holy Spirit throughout the room and in themselves.

The Pastor called John to the front, as a soft instrumental music began over the speaker. John took the microphone and looked over the group of people. John began to speak as they stood there listening in a meditative trance. John was sincere with his faith and love, and he knew that people were suffering and hurting. He knew that life was scary at any age and that everywhere you looked there was always more reality than miracles. There was a lot of insecurity and pain in this room; in any room you walked in the world.

"Sometimes it is so difficult to express what people already know. To repeat what people already heard, and give it strength as if it was the first time they heard it. But unfortunately, we live in a society that it is so easy to yell out, 'I have faith', but so hard to remember that faith without love, is faith in vain. We yell out, 'I believe in Jesus' but we have learned to look the other away and blind to the needs around us. We live in a world that expresses itself in wars, killing lives, whether it's our backyard or across the ocean in the Middle East. We find it easier, to express hate. We find it more entertaining in the media to express hate. We find it more comfortable to speak and act aggressively as long as we are respected, because our society respects aggression and love is for the weak. As long as our faith is without love...our faith is in vain. Hope is dead."

As John finished saying these words the ground in the church began to tremor. Everyone felt it. The lights were flickering on and off. The music stopped people began to get up and walk out. As they walked the tremors on the floor began to get stronger and more intense. For a whole long minute the ground shook as everyone walked out of the church. The Pastor, John and some people helped the older people out. Others held on to the children. It was a quick tremor but long enough to remind us of our mortality. The Pastor stood with his wife and two sons and the entire congregation outside as they waited for the tremble to pass. All of a sudden, about five minutes later a low scale earthquake was felt through Upstate New York. The Grounds shook very hard, some people lost their balance, people were screaming, the church bells rang by themselves, and car alarms were going off. Windows were cracking in different houses and buildings, as walls were cracking. Everyone was holding on to each other; waiting for the earth to stop shaking. The Pastor, John and other men from the church try to calm everyone down. People from houses and buildings were out in the streets. Cars, buses and trucks were all stopping in the middle of the roads. You could see some houses and buildings that were shaken badly; glass and rubble were everywhere. Sirens were heard nearby, as well as miles away.

John stood in the middle of the road with his hands in his pocket. He looked around wondering about the extent of the earthquake. The earthquake was over, but he knew that upstate New York was not the center of earthquake. They only received the outskirt. What kind of damage was created in the areas fully hit by the earthquake? He knew this was significant.

People were crying and shaking. The church was standing and they decided to go back inside. They found that a couple of windows were cracked. There were a couple of big cracks on the walls, but everything else seemed fine. The congregation got in a circle as they began to pray. The Pastor saw that John walked away from the circle and sat himself at the foot of the alter. The Pastor followed him, "John are you alright? You are not going to pray with us?"

"When you live for some time, you learn to read the signs. It grieves me, to see that the time has come for the greatest democracy to exist in the history of the world, to change. This great democracy will change forever. We are getting very close to a new era. An era where the freedom to be a Christian will be gone and we shall be persecuted and killed in the name of Jesus. This earthquake was very significant and by this time tomorrow you will understand what I am talking about. Go pray, Pastor. Pray like you never prayed before."

The President of the United States was yelling, "How bad is the damage?"

Karl yelled back, "We have to get you out of here and onto higher grounds. I have a chopper waiting for you, sir. Let's go!"

"What are you talking about?" The President asked.

"Karl, what do you know?" Jenna asked.

"It seems that in the borderlines of southeast Missouri and southwest Illinois, where the two states meet, there has been an 11.0 Rector Scale Earthquake."

"My God." The President was dumbfounded.

Jenna and Frank did not know what to say.

"We do not know the amount of casualties yet. But the earthquake was felt from Illinois and Missouri down to Mississippi, Louisiana, and parts of Texas. It was felt going across through Kentucky, Tennessee, and South Carolina and up the east coast all the way to Massachusetts. I do not know about Florida and other states. But we are concerned with the ocean and the possibility of major tsunamis off the eastern coast."

"Sir," the Secretary rushed in, "turn on the TV. We have a signal."

A reporter came on the screen. The President and everyone watched dumbfounded.

"This is a helicopter view of our nation at this time. An 11.0 Rector Scale earthquake has basically split the United States in half. From the Great Lakes by the states of Wisconsin and Illinois all the way down through the state of Louisiana. Parts of Wisconsin, Indiana, Iowa, Minnesota, Kentucky, Tennessee, most of Arkansas, basically all of Mississippi, all of Louisiana, and parts of Texas have been destroyed and is under water. We do not know how many lives have been lost. We all pray and look towards the President of this country to see what actions are going to be taken. This is the biggest natural disaster this land has ever experienced."

"Sir, the Coast Guard is already in place throughout the East coast to evacuate the entire coast. Biggest problem we have encountered is the congestions caused by too many people in their vehicles trying to evacuate." Karl stated with urgency.

"Karl, we have to make sure these people are safe! I need to know what's going on at all times!" The President exclaimed.

"Sir, we need take you and your family in the chopper right now to higher grounds in Pennsylvania. We have a cabin over there where you will be safe and are able to run the country. Let's go now, Sir!"

"Sir!" Jenna yelled and everyone turned to her. "The tsunami has begun. It has put the State of Florida under water and gigantic waves are moving up the East Coast. They are trying to evacuate people along the coast as quickly as possible."

Helicopters left Washington DC with The President, his family, his chief advisors, Secret Service, and many others from Capitol Hill. They all flew to higher ground. The President and his crew were taken to a secured cabin located in Pennsylvania.

Two hours later the map of the United States was changed forever. The Earthquake had open the ground from the southern part of Wisconsin to the eastern parts of Texas and the waters from the Gulf of Mexico filled the space, creating a new body of water dividing the country. Louisiana, Alabama and most of Florida were all underwater. From Florida up the East Coast to Main the Coast was completely flooded and changed. The coasts of Georgia, Virginia, South Carolina and North Carolina were destroyed and underwater. But New Jersey, Manhattan, New York City, Washington DC, Staten Island, Long Island, Delaware, were all severely damaged by giant waves. The borders of Massachusetts and Maine were also destroyed. Throughout the nation the news casters cried openly on television, because everyone had lost someone throughout the nation.

The President sat alone in front of a window in a cabin in the mountains of Pennsylvania. His family and advisors were safe. But they all lost family members. He needed time to be alone, somehow collect himself and his thoughts. As he sat there he cried into his hands. America was changed forever and he is supposed to bring it back together.

In a little church in Upstate, New York Pastor Silva, his family, John and the rest of the congregation all were having a vigil. They prayed, they spoke, they consoled each other and they cried together. Many of them lost family members and friends. Some questioned God as they all tightly hung on to their faith. Their lives were changed forever.

CHAPTER NINE

The Voice And The Reason

Prime Minister Taylor sat behind his desk drinking hot tea and studying the chart in front of him. It was a list of different leaders and information pertinent to each of them. His mind quickly went over every detail as if playing a real life chess game. His secretary buzzed him and as she interrupted his concentration he asked absentmindedly, "Yes?"

"Sir," There was a pause, "Sir, it's 'The Voice'."

Prime Minister Taylor sat still and quietly. "The Voice" does not phone very much, but when "The Voice" does there will be something happening. Betsy was a good secretary and followed orders. She never quite understood who "The Voice" was, but she was told that if "The Voice" called it must be announced quickly and put through without delay. Prime Minister Taylor answered, "Thank you. Put him through." As the Prime Minister Taylor picked-up the phone, he apprehensively said, "Hello."

"Prime...Minister...Taylor, how are you?" The Voice asked calmly.

"Excellent, Sir; I hope you are doing well." Prime Minister Taylor answered.

"Yes. There are too many important things going on, Damion. You and I need to put ourselves up-to-date." The Voice said controlling the conversation.

"As you know I had a meeting with some of Europe's leaders..." Taylor was interrupted.

"And?" The Voice demanded.

"France, Germany, Portugal, and Poland all have agreed to help me establish a new European Union. We are supposed to have a second meeting soon to manifest an agreement and details."

"Good. What about the Biochip?" The Voice asked.

"They love the concept. They understand its benefits and they would like to incorporate it into action as soon as possible. If everything goes as planned, most of Europe will have a Biochip in their hands by the end of this year," Taylor answered.

"The money is ready for the investment. You have done well, Damion. What is the problem?" The Voice asked.

"No problem, Sir." Damion answered.

"Damion, no need to worry; you are doing well and, trust me, you are doing a great thing for your country and for those who follow and join you. You will become the central figure of Europe. You and the countries that join you will be protected and, how do they love to say, oh yes, *blessed*." The voice spoke mockingly, but reassuring.

"So, what is the problem?" The Voice insisted.

Taylor took a deep breath, "Spain."

The Voice laughed out-loud, "The money-loving Bulldog."

"He is being very stubborn," Taylor explained.

"I am assuming the attack did not help?" The Voice asked.

"Not only did it not help, but as you know, Spain and Russia have been close allies for years; many Russians go to Spain for vacation. My understanding is that the massacre in Spain killed about three hundred Russians."

"How many Spaniards were killed?" The Voice asked.

"About five hundred." Damion replied.

"The Bulldog did not change his mind?"

"Not at all." Damion answered.

"Stubborn idiot; he is going to get the people in his country killed." The Voice spoke emphatically. "Personally I don't care. But he should." The Voice continued, "And what is Russia saying about all of this?"

"Prime Minister Bogdanovich wants to know what happened and who was behind the act of terrorism."

The Voice asked, "They do not believe the explanation about the civil movement? That the massacre was caused by rebel Spaniards?"

"No." Taylor answered.

The Voice spoke as he was deep in thought, "Prime Minister Viktor Bogdanovich is very smart."

Taylor continued, "He wants answers; he and I have an appointment later today about the European union. As you know he was not able to attend the first meeting. I am sure the conversation about Spain will surface."

"Use the attack in Spain to persuade him to join the Union. The European Allies can protect each other from terrorism. I would love to see the reaction of the Bulldog if Russia joins the Union." The Voice laughed cynically. "Also," The Voice continued, "The Russian Orthodox Church has a good relationship with the Pope. We need to go to The Vatican and convince them of The Biochip."

"The Vatican?" Prime Minister Taylor asked.

"If The Vatican accepts The Biochip, Catholics throughout the world will follow and we will have a large amount of people integrated with the Biochip program. This will also be in conflict with the rest of the Christian community and create confusion."

"I thought we have plans for The Vatican?" Taylor asked.

"We do; nothing has changed. But we will lead astray as many as their blind sheep as possible and create confusion. Then we will follow through with our plans."

"Ingenious," The Voice always manages to humble Prime Minister Taylor.

"Taylor."

"Yes, Sir?"

"You are doing well. Trust me, you are doing well. Before I forget, you will be able to count with Ireland. I am taking care of the IRA for you and they won't be a problem."

Prime Minister Taylor was surprised by these words; but he did not dare to question. The IRA had been a problem for a very long time; since before World War II. The IRA was a group of Irish who did not wish to be part of the United Kingdom anymore. They have always been a problem and now they will unite to the European Union?

"Someone will be contacting you about this matter very soon." The Voice explained.

"Alright Sir, I will be looking forward to the phone call."

"Good-bye," The Voice said.

"Good-bye, Sir," Prime Minister Taylor hung up the phone. Sat for a couple of minutes and noticed that he was wet with sweat from his head to his feet. His hands were trembling. He got up slowly, had a quick scotch and walked to the bathroom to shower.

A couple of hours after Prime Minister Taylor and The Voice were done speaking; a Special News Report caught Taylor's attention. The female broadcaster was giving an update on an occurrence in Syria. "Earlier today Russia bombed Islamic State targets in Syria, at very strategic areas. Twelve trucks carrying oil were destroyed. As well, as part of an oil refinery location which was hit with fifteen long-range cruise missiles that were shot from a war ship at the Caspian Sea. All the targets that were hit were property of ISIS. It is unknown how many casualties were there or the cost of the damage. But the action taken by Russia is seen as retaliation for the terrorist attack that occurred a few days ago in Spain, where 300 vacationing Russians and 500 Spaniards were killed. Some people are questioning the actions of the Prime Minister of Russia, Viktor Bogdonavich, because it was believed that the massacre at Spain happened as a civil movement against the government of Spain and not as an ISIS terrorist attack. We will keep you updated as this story progresses."

Taylor sat quietly as he muted the news. He needed these moments of silence. There was too much bloodshed in the world and he knew that this was just the beginning.

Prime Minister Taylor was once again himself; cold, collected and analytical as he sat in a private dining area with Prime Minister Viktor Bogdonavich from Russia. Viktor was tall, husky and strong; but he was also very analytical and calculating. Viktor was not afraid and he played a very aggressive political game. He believed that when you beat your opponent, he will always return. So, the idea is to destroy your opponent so that you never see him again. Viktor would only let you know what he wanted you to know and you would never know what he is thinking.

The best china, the best crystals and the best silverware were all laid out on the table. Viktor loved steak medium rare, bake potatoes and red wine. Prime Minister Taylor loved his filet mignon with sauce, steamed green vegetables bathed in garlic butter and wine. They were past the complimentary and the respectful small talk in front of everyone and now they were alone. Taylor looked at Viktor in the eyes and brought up the true reason for the meeting.

"Why did you do it?" Taylor asked.

Viktor looked at Taylor, knowing what he was referring to and having no reason to play ignorant, he knew that he deserved an honest answer. Viktor liked Taylor and had great respect for him; he knew he was genuinely fare and reverent. Forgetting the fact that Taylor always got along with the United States, a country Viktor despised, Viktor still had great admiration for the Prime Minister of England.

Viktor looked into Taylor's eyes and said in a low baritone voice, "I had three hundred reasons."

Taylor stopped eating and looked at Viktor as he processed his answer in his mind. "The vengeance of three hundred lives killed wrongfully while on vacation, is a very good reason. But," Taylor made sure that he had Viktor's undivided attention before he continued, "but there is a weakness in your explanation, my friend. It is known that the massacre was caused by a civil movement in Spain. It was a statement against the government. Nothing indicated that it was an ISIS terrorist attack."

Viktor looked at Taylor as he finished swallowing his food. "I do not believe that story. I read the reports and I do not believe them. I am convinced that it was those snakes of the Middle East, ISIS that slimed themselves into Spain and created the blood-shed that killed innocent people. They are cowards!" Viktor spoke with hate in his face.

Taylor listened attentively as he took his sip of wine.

"The incident has been reported with very concrete and strong facts. As the shooting was happening the men were heard yelling in Spanish. Also, one of the attackers was killed and he had Spanish documents; he was described as citizen from Spain."

"I understand," Viktor continued, "I know what the report says. I do not know how it was done. These European countries are infiltrated with aliens from Syria and other parts of the Middle East. France, Spain and other countries have aliens from the Middle East that are not there to find a better life or escape from a degrading regime; they are there to camouflage there true purpose of creating bloodshed for Islam. I have to follow my gut feeling on this one and I know that somehow, ISIS was involved."

"Prime Minister Rojas, your friend, has a lot of enemies..." Taylor started saying.

"Every true good leader has many enemies." Viktor interrupted.

"I respect your friendship with Rojas." Taylor continued, "But we cannot allow friendship to blind us to death. Rojas has made a lot of enemies and Spain is in a verge of a civil war. I feel that the Spaniards as well as the Russians are at great risk being in Spain. The Spaniards you cannot help, but the Russians you can. I wanted to help Rojas. But he refuses to join the European Union."

Viktor listened attentively, "I know how Rojas could be. He is a good strong leader. People do not like him because he does not put up with nonsense. Sometimes the most popular decision is not the best one; and a true leader has to know when to be unpopular."

"Correct," Taylor agreed, "that is why he has enemies and that is why you have to protect your people."

Taylor continued as if changing the conversation, "Let's say that you are right. That it was ISIS and not a civil movement. That is why I wanted Spain to join the Europe Union and that is why I am inviting you to join us too. Now Rojas refuses; but I implore you to consider how strong we can be together in the fight against terrorism and how rewarding it would be if we all extend that union into business and economically. All I am asking you to do is to read our proposed Manifesto and then give me your feedback."

Viktor was very deep in thought, he asked, "Who has agreed to join this new European Union?"

"At this point France, Poland, Germany and Portugal have joined us. I am waiting to hear from Norway, Sweden and Finland. We will create a European Military movement against terrorism that the Middle East will realize that Europe has united as one country ready to fight them. Europe will become like one nation, but keep its distinctive customs."

"I see," Viktor said pondering and dissecting everything he heard.

"All I know is that ISIS is depending on us to stay divided. Divided we will lose this battle one by one."

"I understand. I hate these dogs so much. Syn Sukil!" Viktor spoke with anger.

"Viktor my friend, please join us. We have the same enemy." Taylor asked very sincerely.

Viktor was quiet.

Taylor continued, "I forgot to mention to you, Ireland wishes to join our European Union."

Viktor's forehead wrinkled, "Ireland?"

"Yes," Taylor answered.

"I find it hard to believe; but very impressive if true. Ireland has been trying to break from the United Kingdom for a long time and now it will join you on this project?"

"The world has changed, my friend. It is no longer a world of "ME". It is "WE" against "THEM" and "THEM" are terrorists; individualism is suicidal."

"Fine," Viktor spoke seriously, "I will read your proposal. If I like what I read, we will speak further about the matter."

"That is all I ask, Prime Minister Bogdanovich." Taylor answered with a grin.

"Now, what about Spain?" Taylor asked.

"Spain and our country understand each other. We both come from monarchies and poverty. We have both have revolted and experience civil wars. We have both lived under dictatorships and survived. We have both been stronger than our challenges and the challenges have been many. I communicate very well with Rojas. Our childhoods were very similar and we have achieved levels of power. It is difficult to get to the top; it is impossible to stay there. All we can do is fight to stay as long as we can. I respect my friend, Rojas. I will read your proposal, but I will let you know, my friend, Rojas has his own mind. If I find out that anyone in the Middle East, ISIS, Europe or even the United States infringes in the life of the Spaniards; I will override any opinion of a Europe Union and declare war on that country. Are we clear?"

"We are clear," Taylor answered looking at Viktor's eyes, "That is why we want Spain to join us; so that we can *ALL* protect Spain."

Viktor stared at Taylor and Taylor at Viktor.

Viktor picked up his wine and said, "Ura!"

"Cheers!" Taylor replied.

◆❖◆

The next day Prime Minister Taylor sat in his private room having a scotch, when the phone rang.

"Hello." Taylor answered.

"Hello, Prime Minister Taylor, this is President Garret Byrne how are you, my friend?"

Taylor was dumbfounded, "President Byrne, what a pleasant surprise, sir. How are things in Ireland?"

"Very well, thank you. I apologize for the short notice. Hope I am not interrupting you."

"Nonsense, I will always have time to chat with you." Taylor said with a smile.

"I was wondering if we could get together soon to chat about the Europe Union and the Biochip?"

"I will get to you my Manifesto. It explains our proposal for the New European Union and the Biochip. After you read it, we could get together and I would be happy to answer your questions and listen to any proposals or ideas of your own." Taylor explained.

"Excellent! I will wait for it with enthusiasm. It will be a pleasure for us to work together." President Byrne spoke energetically.

"Yes, indeed, sir."

As Prime Minister Taylor hung up the phone, he was not sure what just happened and he was not sure he wanted to know. But he knew "The Voice" had something to do with the big change in Ireland. North Western Europe and Russia were coming together as one and he, Prime Minister Taylor, son of Syrian immigrants, raised by adopting English parents, who went from poverty to high class to Prime Minister, is in the middle of it all.

CHAPTER TEN

Walking Among the Mines

Prime Minister Taylor was in his office sitting in front of his computer with head-phones on his head ready to speak with other European leaders that were part of the New European Union. Every European leader was in his personal office, in front of their computers with all the other leaders on the monitor screen. They can all see each other, as well as hear and partake in the conversation just like if they were all in the same room.

"Everyone," Prime Minister Taylor began, "I like to welcome all of you to the first official meeting of the New European Union. As we speak our computers will automatically record the meeting's minutes. Therefore, we will not need a secretary and these conversations will be confidential and only available to us through our personal computers. Every recorded conversation will be kept in a file that will only be opened with a pass word known to the owner of the computer. Do we agree?"

Everyone simultaneously agreed.

"I am pleased to announce that the New European Union consist of," Prime Minister Taylor continued, "President Dubois from France, President Fischer from Germany, President Barbo from Portugal, President Adamik from Poland, President Byrne from Ireland, Prime Minister Elizabeth Stensby from Norway, Prime Minister Thorngren from Sweden, President Saarela from Finland, and of course yours truly, Prime Minister Taylor from England. My friends, we are the New European Union, we are the powers of Europe and we are gathering with the sole purpose to protect Europe from any terrorist or enemy, to ensure the right to a safe and proper life of our citizens, and to advance technologically and financially our countries into a better future; as it is written in our Manifest. I greet you all and I welcome you."

Everyone greeted each other and was thankful to be at the meeting. In all sincerity they all wanted what was best for Europe and their countries.

Dubois quickly went on to ask a question, "Thank you, I too welcome everyone and I do hope that our union is a success. Excuse me Prime Minister Taylor; do we have any word on Prime Minister Rojas?"

Taylor tried very hard not to show his annoyance at the question as he answered Dubois with a smile, "Unfortunately, Prime Minister Rojas has not been able to recognize the importance of our Union at this time. I am truly hoping that in the near future as he sees the progress of Europe and our nations that he reconsiders his position and values what we are doing here. When he decides to join us, the door will be open and we shall welcome him."

"He has always been a stubborn bull," Fischer stated as a fact.

Everyone snickered and laughed mildly; except Taylor.

"Fischer." Taylor said softly.

"I am just stating the facts." Fischer said with a smile.

"I rather that we take the time to speak about the important matters that we have to resolve and not about the few that lack the vision to see the future that is near and the need that Europe has to prepare in order to survive." Taylor spoke seriously. Taylor quickly changed the conversation, "I feel the first thing we need to resolve is the incorporation of the Micro-biochip in Europe; questions, statements, ideas, anything?"

President Byrne from Ireland asked, "Do we feel that the Biochip really needs to become a part of our lives? Honestly it is a foreign object in the human body; do we feel that the pros of the Biochip in our bodies are far more advantages than the cons? Is it really worth this drastic change of life? Don't misunderstand me, I am not against it, but are we sure of what we are doing?"

Taylor answered slowly, "The Biochip is the future and the future is here. The Micro-biochip has been tested and at no time has it shown any signs of bacterial danger in the body. It is safe."

President Fischer from Germany added, "I agree with Prime Minister Taylor, the future is here. Personally, I am tired that when it comes to Space, weapons, technology, and medicine I feel that Europe is always behind the United States and Russia; when in fact we know, that hundreds of years ago Europe was the center of many innovating ideas that changed the world. Europe needs to take the lead in the Micro-biochip and be ahead of the game."

"I have been following the studies of the Micro-biochip and there are great advantages." Prime Minister Stensby from Norway spoke, "I always wanted the Chip to become part of our society. We will be able to do our banking, have our medical records readily available, children will be safe from being taken from their parents, they can be used as passports, and the chips can be used as credit cards or bankcards. We will be able to keep better control of society and even prisoners that escape or are allowed to go back in society. The advantages are endless and what we are planning to do with Europe; the way we want to unite across the borders it is the perfect timing and technology to help us reach our goals."

President Adamik from Poland broke in with a question, "This all sound good and everything, but I do have a concern. What is going to prevent people from going up to people with the Chip in the skin of their hands and basically steal it; and have all the person's information and access to their accounts?"

"I was wondering about that myself," President Byrne from Ireland said with great concern.

Prime Minister Thornga added, "The way things are nowadays, they would cut the hand off to use the Chip."

Some people reacted with sounds of repulsion at the comment.

Thornga continued, "Sorry to be so descriptive but it's the truth. You see these animals in the Middle East online beheading people; it is a lot easier to cut off a hand."

"People please calm down," Taylor took over the conversation. "Your questions about the prevention of theft towards the Micro-biochip are very valid. Let me explain, first of all everything that Prime Minister Stensby was talking about the use of the Biochip is correct. Bankcard, passport, medical records, children's safety, etc., etc., the list is infinite and it will change our world. It is one of the most life changing discoveries across civilization that we have seen in a long time. Life will never be the same as this invention is put into circulation and weeks turn into months, months into years and years turn into new generations that are born already with the Micro-biochip.

Secondly, let me explain that the Micro-biochip comes with an anti-theft device that is guaranteed 100%. Every person that gets the Micro-biochip in the hand will also receive a tattooed infrared number on the forehead. This number cannot be seen by the naked eye. Where ever you go, to the store, the doctor's office, hospital, airport anywhere that you use the Micro-biochip, you first must put your forehead close to infrared device attached to the machine being used, the infrared device will read the number on your forehead and it must coincide with the number in the Chip; If it doesn't the person will have a problem. The number will not be seen by the naked eye and people will have on their foreheads a mark that is nothing more than a small area of skin that looks a shade darker than the rest of their skin. It's a mark that after a while everyone will be used to it."

President Byrne from Ireland spoke-up, "I feel that it is great that we take the initiative in this project. That Europe unites in this technological life-changing event, as well as financially and in declaring war against terrorism."

"Let's not get ahead of ourselves and start talking about other issues like terrorism. We will be touching that subject in a few minutes. I like to remind everyone", Prime Minister Taylor continued, "that in the Manifesto that I sent out to each of you explains how the cost of the making and the buying of these Micro-bio Chips will be handled. It is very simple, if anyone has any questions pertaining to this, I will be more than happy to answer your questions and clarify any doubts."

There were no questions.

"Also, very important to keep in our minds that every time that the Micro-Biochip belonging to a country is used any-where around the world 3% of the cost of the transaction goes to the country's account in the new World Bank. That, my friends, is a lot of revenues for our countries. It is the greatest investment that our countries could make." Prime Minister Taylor explained.

Everyone applauded with agreement.

"That money can in turn be used in your country as you wish."

THE TIME HAS COME

President Barbo from Portugal asked a question, "What would in fact happen if someone removes the chip?"

"I assume that they would feel a lot of pain." Taylor answered humorously.

"Nothing, but they will make it very difficult for themselves to access their own accounts. It wouldn't make sense."

"I heard that the Chip would have a poisonous mechanism that would be triggered if people try to remove it." President Barbo insisted.

Taylor smiled, "You shouldn't believe everything you read." Taylor was told by The Voice that that would be the only correct answer if the question arises. Taylor wondered what the truth is.

Taylor changed the conversation, "I am very excited about this; every one of us will be receiving 500,000 Micro-biochips so that we may begin to introduce the Chip in our countries. One banking firm which has many branches throughout Europe has already agreed to invest in the infrared equipment and to make the necessary changes at the bank machines that this investing financial company has throughout Europe, in order to help put the Micro-biochip in circulation in our countries."

Everyone was excited and started to speak at the same time. Taylor observed the excitement of the group on the screen and surrendered the microphone to the group to allow them to speak among themselves and watched their excitement grow. He could not help but to smile realizing that his dream has begun to materialize.

Prime Minister Stensby spoke up, she was very serious and focused, being the only woman in the group she had the necessity to be not only respected but to be taken serious when she spoke, "I do have a question; what are we planning to do when people or certain groups begin to refuse their participation in the use of the Micro-biochip? I have read that Christians all around are against this idea."

"I also have heard of *all* kinds of different people that do not feel comfortable with the idea of placing the chip in their hand; but to be honest any time something major and life changing is introduced people are afraid. Human nature does not like change, especially if they feel that it is something they don't need. Therefore, we do nothing. If they refuse, we let it be, but we make sure we have their information. Once we have a list throughout Europe, we will see how many are true Christians and how many are just uncomfortable with the idea of the Chip and we will figure out what would be the correct course of action."

"We cannot allow anything to slow down our plans. The Micro-biochip will resurrect Europe and the revenues will create a prosperous Europe like we haven't seen since World War II. This is *our* moment; I say at all cost we must agree to stick together with the goal to unite Europe and to grow financially." President Fischer from Germany spoke up with enthusiasm and everyone verbalized their agreement.

Taylor smiled as he was surprised to hear Fischer speaking with such enthusiasm. Taylor continued, "Everyone will receive the Micro-Biochips and instructions to set up stations to begin implant procedures, which by the way are very simple."

Everyone was applauding and speaking with great enthusiasm.

Taylor continued, "We are running out of time. We must proceed to the second agenda of our meeting. I am sure that everyone read my proposal in the Manifest pertaining to ISE, which stands for Intelligent Service of Europe."

President Byrne from Ireland asked, "Yes, actually very interesting. Would they be more like police, military or like undercover?"

President Fischer from Germany spoke up, "In actuality I feel that a combination of undercover and military will be more suitable for our war against terrorism."

Taylor surprised at Fischer's statement, but with complete agreement, "Correct, the military portion will be trained to act in a split second against any type of terrorism, while the undercover will blend among the regular people and be very observant as they too will be trained in what to look for and how to act in case of a terrorist action."

President Adamyk from Poland asked, "Is the ISE going to be allowed to move freely among our countries or are they going to be assigned to their own country?"

"The ISE," Taylor continued, "will have the ability to move around the nine countries that are represented here and any other country that join us in the future. The authority given to the ISE will come from the nine of us and no other local law or Interpol or anything will have authority over ISE. Do we agree?"

Everyone understood and loved the idea.

"You think Interpol will accept what we intend to do with ISE?" Dubois asked.

"It does not matter what Interpol or the UN or the United States or anyone else thinks, the New European Union along with ISE will be in charge of the European territory and the world will have to adapt to us. Interpol, the UN, they all had their chance to keep us safe. Dubois, have they kept us safe?" Taylor asked with emotion.

"No," Dubois answered with hate in his face.

"What happened in France? What happened in Spain? This can happen to any one of us; enough already!" Taylor exclaimed.

Taylor continued, "The UN will be notified about our plans; but they will understand that we are not asking for permission, but that we are informing them of our position. The UN is outdated, the world has changed too much and they do not move aggressively or quick enough to meet the needs Europe. We will leave up to the discretion of each country as to whether you wish to maintain a representative in the United Nations."

President Barbo from Portugal spoke, "I feel that the UN is outdated. They were a great organization until the world has become bathed with blood from terrorist attacks and they have not been able to form any aggressive plan to protect our countries. But I also, feel that unless they try to stop our union, we should maintain our representatives on their chair in the UN; as long as our representatives realize that they are there to inform us as to what is going on in the UN and to inform the UN that we stand firm by our laws and not by any other."

"I couldn't say it better myself." Taylor agreed.

"Each of you will pick five-hundred men and you will be given an address in Germany, where you will send these men, and in the meantime President Fischer will begin to prepare for an intense training where these men will learn what is expected of them as ISE Agents and how to combat terrorism."

Taylor did not have a choice; The Voice had chosen Fischer for the training.

President Fischer jumped in, "We are ready with the program and the place for forty days of intense training. When these men leave the camp they will be taken back to their country to meet with you and they will be ready to follow your orders and you will be ready to incorporate ISE. When these men return to you, we ask that each of you have another 500 men to send to Germany for training. We will do this four times and very soon we will have 18,000 fully trained ISE Agents throughout Europe, who sole purpose will be to protect our citizens."

Taylor was surprised that Fischer was so prepared for the training. They had only talked about the training recently and there is no way that in that short time President Fischer would have prepared so much, so quickly. Taylor felt that Fischer was keeping something from him.

"Thank you, President Fischer." Taylor stated as he watched him.

"Any questions anyone?" Taylor asked.

"Yes," Adamik from Poland spoke, "Why does President Fischer from Germany get to train our men for ISE? I don't mean to insult anyone."

Taylor thought to himself, good question.

"My military record speaks for myself and any one of you is welcomed to come and watch our training." Fischer answered.

Taylor knew that Fischer was chosen by The Voice. When Taylor asked The Voice why, the subject was changed and never touched again. Now Taylor was wondering how Fischer knew so much about the training. All this time Taylor was under the impression that he was the only one in contact with The Voice. He got a sick feeling to his stomach at the thought that The Voice spoke to someone else in this room. How many in this room and what did they talk about?

Taylor never forgot the first phone call from The Voice. It was a Sunday in the middle of the summer and Taylor was home with his wife and his three year old son. The phone rang and it was The Voice, "Hello."

"Hello. Who is this?" Prime Minister Taylor asked.

"*Do not worry about who this is. Let's just say I am The Voice. Your little boy Michael seems to be having a good time in your yard.*"

Taylor looked outside past the living room glass doors. He slowly stated to walk outside.

"*How do you know my son is outside? Who are you?*" *Taylor asked wide eyed with fear.*

"*Listen to me. Leave the questions to me and just listen. First, I would stop walking if I were you. There are three landmines in your backyard where your son is now playing. I suggest that you very carefully walk to your son and bring him into your house and place him safely on your black leather sofa in the living room.*" *Taylor listened quietly; his forehead wrinkled. The Voice continued, "Then call the bomb squad. Work carefully and quickly. If you don't it will be your son's life. The next time I call you, be prepared to listen." He then hung up.*

Slowly Taylor stepped outside drenched in sweat, not knowing where to stand. Taking each step slowly and carefully; afraid of each step being the last one. He picked up Michael in his arms and he hugged him firmly as he tried to trace his steps walking backwards and back into the house. When the bomb squat came they checked Taylor's entire backyard and they only found one land mine all the way by the fence on the right side of the yard by the tree; set up and ready to blow up if stepped on. Taylor received the message from The Voice loud and clear, The Voice knows who he is, he knows where he lives, he knows his family, and he was able to get in there without a trace and set up a bomb. They were not able to find one small lead in the search of his entire house. Taylor was not able to trace the phone call from The Voice. He tried at the beginning a few times, to no avail. Since then Taylor's life changed forever and The Voice became a part of his life.

Taylor looked at his group on the monitor as they talked to each other and for the first time he wondered who else from this group has contact with The Voice? Who else on that screen does he need to fear and not trust. For now he knew that he couldn't trust President Fischer from Germany; but he had to continue his relationship like he did. He felt in his stomach the same sick feeling he felt walking in his backyard with the landmine to save his boy. He must stay strong and sharp and not allow his insecurity to show.

"Thank you, everyone. If there are no questions, I think we could conclude this meeting. Let's agree to put our plans into motion," Taylor stated.

Everyone agreed and began to sign off. The first meeting of the European Union was over.

Early the next day, Prime Minister Taylor arrived at Italy and went straight to the Vatican as the sunrise spread throughout the monumental architecture. He was there to meet with Cardinal Scarpato in the courtyard of the Vatican. They met and shook hands. *"Buongiorno,* Prime Minister Taylor," the Cardinal spoke.

"Buongiorno," Taylor answered back. He liked the Italian language. Personally he founded more interesting than French. Taylor always thought that French may be the language of love, but Italians can say whatever is on their minds and make it sound good.

"Thank you for meeting with me, Cardinal." Taylor began the conversation. The *barista* came by serving Puerto Rican café.

"Zucchero?" The barista asked.

"Due." Taylor answered as he put two fingers up and the *barista* went on to put two lumps of sugar in his café.

"Grazie," Taylor said.

"Prego," the *barista* replied and left.

"Cardinal," Taylor began his conversation, "You and I have known each other for some time. I think about ten years now."

"Yes, we go back and we have had a good relationship," Cardinal agreed.

"We have made a lot of successful investments together." Taylor noted as he watched the Cardinal.

"We have made a lot of money together." The Cardinal said smiling.

Cardinal Scarpo was a thin light skin man, he had a very pointy nose, very nervous eyes, he wore glasses at the tip of his nose, and he always seemed very jumpy. He always had dark circles under his eyes and was very anemic. It was almost as though he entered the house of God, but the peace of God never entered him. He was a very shrewd business man and he made a lot of money for the Vatican throughout his years of serving God. Taylor always smiled at that little piece of information, he knew the Cardinal well and Taylor always found him somewhat of an irony.

"Cardinal, in the past you and I have had strange conversations and we made plans that were out of the ordinary thinking of the Vatican. But we always did everything with our hearts in the right place; for the good of God's creatures."

"Yes, of course my son. God works in mysterious ways and it is more important for the heart to be right with God, even if the actions are questionable; than if we take good actions with questionable intentions. *Intenzioni sono tutto.*"

"Yes," Taylor replied, "Intentions are everything. I am glad you feel that way; because what I am about to propose to you I do with very good intentions.

I am coming to invite the Vatican to incorporate the Micro-biochip into your life." Taylor waited for a reaction.

The Cardinal looked at Taylor, squinting his eyes and with a confuse expression in his face. Like those moments when you have no idea what to say back to a person, so you repeat what you heard.

"Micro-biochip?"

"I know that you know what a Micro-biochip is. I also, know that you are the Senior Cardinal. You have a strong hold and lots of secrets on every person of God in this place. I need you to push your power and have the Vatican invest and participate in the Micro-biochip."

The Cardinal was quiet for a second as he collected his thoughts. "Taylor, I like you. We are friends and we have a history together. But..." The Cardinal searched for the words, "why would we agree to do this? The Micro-biochip has a lot of ethical questions and I do not know if it would be in the best interest of the Vatican to get involved."

"Antoni," the Cardinal realized that Taylor did not call him Cardinal, "do not talk to me about ethics. You guys have right here, at the Vatican, a wall twenty feet high going all around your premises. You guys are not trying to keep anybody out; like the Pope said years ago about that US president candidate who wanted to build a wall on the border of Mexico and called him a non-Christian. No, you guys don't want to keep anybody out! You guys don't want anybody to see what is going on inside. Because if people could see inside the Vatican...WOW!

If these Walls of Jericho could speak, what a tale they would tell."

The Cardinal was tightening his lips, listening to Taylor, waiting to see what he had to say. If Taylor was speaking like this it was because he had something up his sleeve.

"All right, I am listening." The Cardinal spoke calmly.

"Before you spoke about, what *interest* the Vatican can possibly have on the Micro-biochip. Let me talk to you about interest." Taylor began to explain. "When you guys invest in the Micro-biochip and help us to go public with this, the Vatican will receive 3% of every transaction that any Catholic throughout the world does with the Micro-biochip. The Micro-Biochip will be worldwide, a global business and its revenues will be in the billions of dollars. We are ready to put together a contract with the Vatican and Italy; your *circo degli angelis* will see more money than you have ever imagined. Even more money on top of what you guys already have. You will be helping us, The European Union, because the Christians are against the Micro-biochip and they will confuse the minds of the Catholics. But when the Catholics see that the Vatican accepts the Micro-biochip we are all going to make a lot of money. The Vatican will make a lot of money and you will be known as the Cardinal that brought the biggest and most lucrative business deal ever made in the Vatican. There is a tremendous Catholic population out there. Do you understand me?"

"This sounds very good and definitely lucrative. As good as it sounds; I have to make sure that it doesn't blow up in my face. There are a lot of negative beliefs about the Micro-biochip that go against everything that *supposedly* we stand for, here at the Vatican. If I bring this up and I can't convince them, what would happen to my reputation and career?" The Cardinal spoke defensively.

"Well, let me give you one more incentive. It is no secret that the Muslims, ISIS and other groups of Muslims in the Middle East want to blow up the Vatican to dust. As soon as they can or make the necessary plans, they will."

Taylor was looking in the Cardinal's eyes.

"They want to destroy this place. It's no secret. The Micro-biochip is a big pie and there is money for everyone. The Vatican can be a big resource because of the Catholics. There is a lot of money to be made from Catholics all around the world wearing the chip. If you make this happen, I assure you no Muslim is going to touch the Vatican."

The Cardinal smiled, "You are trying to scare the Vatican? Have you lost your mind? I always had more respect for you than that."

"I am not trying to scare you." Taylor spoke calm and collected. "I am trying to save you." Taylor got up to leave, "Cardinal, Grazie per il café, arrivederci."

"Do you think you could come to the 'House of God' and put fear in our hearts?"

Prime Minister Taylor stopped and looked at the Cardinal, "If God is truly here; history shows that he has not made anyone immortal on this Earth; which means, he will watch the Muslims blow this place up. The question is, not if your faith will save you; the question is, do you have enough faith that knowing the things the Vatican has done *behind* these walls, would you be ready to face your maker?"

Taylor spoke as he walked away.

"The times are changing, Cardinal. These are the end of time as we know it; try the Book of Revelations. Arrivaderci, Cardinal. You know where to find me."

Taylor walked out of the Vatican, realizing that every time he left this place, he had the same sick feeling in his stomach that he had when he was afraid of stepping on a landmine.

CHAPTER ELEVEN

The Upheaval

The President of the United States sat in his office, in the wooden cabin, secluded in the Pennsylvania woods. Karl Garret walked into the office, his sleeves rolled up, top button untied and his tie knot loose. Like always energetic and on top of everything.

"You have to look at the screen." He yelled at the President as he grabbed the remote to turn the large plasma television on the wall.

"What now?" The President asked with frustration.

"There has been an earthquake in California, sir," Karl explained.

The President looked at Carl with disbelief. The screen was turned on and a helicopter was showing an air shot of California, as the reporter spoke, "The massive earthquake of a week ago which started at the border lines where Illinois and Missouri meet was felt all the way southward to Texas and created an opening with the depth of 4,000 feet, compare that to the Grand Canyon which is 6,000 feet; the opening is 10 miles wide in comparison to the Grand Canyon which is 18 miles wide. When the earthquake reached the Gulf of Mexico, water from the Gulf ran into the massive opening and created a body of water dividing the Eastern part of the United States with the western part. The earthquake also moved eastward dividing Arkansas, Mississippi, Alabama, Georgia and South Carolina and other southern states from the northern part of the country. If that was not enough the massive earthquake created a tsunami along the east coast that has covered with water most of Florida and most of the borders of the states along the East coast. Manhattan and States like New Jersey, Connecticut, and Rhode Island are dealing with massive flooding. We have not been able to complete any statistics of death toll or damage. Now, when we thought it was over, today a massive 10.3 Rector Scale earthquake has occurred in California. During the last week the residence of California has felt aftershocks of last week's earthquake, but nothing else. Today it was a full blown massive earthquake that started in Los Angeles and it was felt throughout Beverly Hills, and Hollywood. Land marks like the Chinese Theater, The Walk of Fame and The Hollywood Bowl are all destroyed. Route 1 past Malibu and heading up to almost San Francisco it is a disaster area. Houses built on cliff sides have become rubble as they have fallen to the ground. PCH or Pacific Coast Highway has been destroyed in many places along the coast. Many people driving on this road have crashed and died. Famous beach areas like Santa Monica Pier, Malibu, Coronado and others are all gone. Massive destruction and an unimaginable death toll wait to be heard in the conclusion to this monster of an earthquake; that we hope it is finally over."

The President watched in terror. As the helicopter camera showed Santa Ana in Orange, Santa Cruz, coast of Monterey, Santa Barbara, Ventura, Santa Monica all destroyed and under water. Expensive houses turning into rubble. Bodies floating, as the current took them away they were sucked into the under current or slammed into a floating house. The people were desperately trying to evacuate the coast. A tsunami was definitely going to hit the coast. It was a question of when and how strong.

"Now Sir, the Red Cross is helping across the country with food and water. Also, the National Guard is helping out and we are already sending The National Guard out to California. But we have a major problem with the south." Karl explained.

"What is it?" The President asked.

"Groups in Texas have united and enticed other groups in Oklahoma, Arizona, New Mexico, Arkansas, Mississippi, Tennessee, and other southern states to stand against the government. Basically, they are saying that our government can no longer protect the people of this country and they are creating a movement to separate from the union." Karl spoke the facts and you could feel the anger in his voice. He believed in the President and he felt bad that all this was happening during his term.

"What exactly are these groups doing?" The President asked.

"The group is compiled mostly of very angry 'Red Necks' and KKK members." Karl stated.

The President's face was surprised as he opened his eyes wide and pulled back his head. "What? KKK! What the hell year are we in?"

"They are burning houses that belong to blacks and Spanish people. They are giving people options; if they are black to go across the "crack" up North and if they are Spanish to move back to the South or up North; they don't care. But if they stay they will have to respect the laws of segregation that will be put into action within the next month. They have shot and actually burned people in Texas. All over the state they have the Confederate flag and the movement is led by a gentleman by the name of William Austin, some billionaire with oil. Who actually believe that he can bring back the Civil War and this time win."

At that time Jenna and Frank walked in and were listening to Carl with disbelief. Right after them the Vice-President walked in, always with a smile on his face; "Good-morning, everyone!"

Jenna and Frank said good morning right away; Carl hardly paid attention to him. Carl did not trust him and they had had an argument a few weeks ago that ended with Carl saying to the Vice-President, "If you are ever President I will either quit or kill myself."

And the Vice-President answered with a smile, "I will be pleased to except either one."

Since then they have never spoken.

"Good morning, George," the President said, "Please sit down."

"Sir, I am very sorry to hear what is happening down South. Even though you know I am from Tennessee, I do not agree with this movement and I will do anything in my power to help you bring order back to the country." The Vice-President stated looking at the President in the eyes.

"I know, but nonetheless we have a problem and we must confront it and fix it rapidly." The President answered.

The President raised his hand and spoke up, "Now George and everyone, I need you all to be silent and listen to me. More than ever we must put our differences aside and work together. I am aware of the South, the East Coast, California, and the center of the country. I am aware of the millions that have died. I am aware of the geographical changes and I am aware of the ignorant groups that we have out there that are trying to take advantage of the situation, exploited, so that they can play their silly political games, instead of uniting and helping one another. I am aware of the KKK. I am very sad that in my term as President all hell has broken loose. But I am more angry than sad. Our country is in upheaval. That is why I have made a decision. I will explain to you now and to congress this afternoon and tonight I will address the Nation."

"What is it, Sir?" Karl asked. Everyone listened quietly.

"We are calling every troop abroad home. We are declaring Martial Law across The United States of America and we will spread our Coast Guard and troops throughout the Nation." President stated.

"Sir, on your address to the Nation you will have to be very clear as to the meaning of Martial Law. It has not been used in the United States since the Civil War and even then, even though Martial Law ideals were put into action, Martial Law itself was never declared. It was a tactic used by Abraham Lincoln to take control of the situation," Ken explained.

"Well I will explain it," the President stated seriously, "The Constitution of the United States will be suspended. No one will have any rights. No freedom of speech, no freedom of press, no freedom of assembly. If we feel that someone is acting against the United States they will be arrested. If they resist arrest they will be shot. Since the South has created this uproar we will be stopping all government financial help in the southern states. No pensions or Social Security and no welfare. These people are going to have to provide financial assistance at a state level and we will see how much the state can help without the support of the Federal Government. Everything will go back to normal only when the Nation is stable once again.

The South will not be tolerated. We do not move backwards only forward and no KKK group or any other will be tolerated. People let's bring our boys back home and this plan will be in effect starting tomorrow morning."

"Sir," The Vice-President spoke up, "we have American Soldiers doing very important work throughout the Middle East and Europe, if we bring them back home, the work there will be unfinished and we will leave these countries vulnerable to terrorism. You think it's a good idea to bring them all back?"

"The country is in upheaval! The boys are coming back, we will have Martial Law and this country will once again be united. We will concern ourselves with home." The President answered.

The President looked at Karl, "Get the wheels in motion."

"Yes, Sir," Karl answered as he left with Frank and Jenna.

The Vice-President got close to the President, "Mr. President, we need to talk alone."

The President gave George his attention. The President liked George a lot and he trusted him, unlike Karl.

"Mr. President, imposing Martial Law was a great idea, but you need to take it a step further. Once Martial Law is removed these clowns are going to go back to their way of thinking. Trust me I know, I am from the South. I know how they think down there." The Vice-President insisted.

"Alright, what do you suggest?" The President asked.

"Prime Minister Taylor from England is doing a wonderful project in Europe." Vice-President began.

"I know he is uniting Europe." President added.

"More than that, he is implementing the Micro-biochip throughout Europe and is slowly having a strong hold in the problems with Terrorism and the Market. I feel that if we implement the Micro-biochip in the US we will be able to take control of the population without them realizing that we are. We need to change our tactics in order to control a Nation divided by ideals and geographically."

"That's interesting Karl and I have been considering implementing the Biochip. You two have a lot in common, I don't stand how come you guys do not get alone?" The President stated.

"Sir, he doesn't like me. I have no problem with him." The Vice-President stated.

"I like the idea. I am putting you in charge of the project." The President stated, "And try to work things with Karl. He has a strong pull on the Senate. Stronger than you and I. He is very helpful when it comes to handling them."

"I am actually glad you told me that. I will, Sir." The Vice-President smiled. Sometimes in war you need to make friends with our enemies; at least for as long as you need them, The Vice-President thought to himself.

Hours later The President of the United States in agreement with the Senate, declared Martial Law throughout the Nation as of the first of the month; with the goal of restoring the country back to order. All rights were removed and anyone caught speaking or acting against the government will be considered an act of treason and will be treated accordingly. In the meeting with the Senate or in the address to the Nation the President did not mention the second part of the plan, the Micro-biochip.

The people listening at home were surprised and angry. They were not aware that the President had the power to take such action. In the south they were very upset and groups were ready to go to war and continued with their plans of segregation and deportation. The President was firm in his decision and thinking; there will be no civil war. He promised himself that he will not allow it to get that far. This poisonous plant will be cut at the roots, before it may blossom.

Later that night, the Vice-President sat in his office as he waited to receive a phone call. The phone rang, "Hello."

"Good-evening, Vice-President; how are you this evening?" The Voice asked.

"I am doing fine, Sir. Everything according to plan. The south has been instigated into a civil war, Martial Law has been imposed across the Nation and the President has accepted the idea of the Micro-biochip." Vice-President answered.

"Excellent. I will begin the process for you to have easy access to the Micro-biochip and you will get in contact with Prime Minister Taylor. The entire operation will seem as to be implemented by him. Understood?" The Voice asked.

"Yes, Sir," The Vice-President answered.

"Great. Mr. Vice-President, you have kept your side of the bargain and I will keep mine, as soon as I see Martial Law imposed upon the people. It's pleasure doing business with you, Mr. Vice-President." The Voice stated.

"Likewise, Sir," The Vice-President answered and they hung-up.

CHAPTER TWELVE

Ideals and Truths

The tall thin figure with the long black coat over the black turtleneck walked along Canalside in Buffalo, New York. As he walked he watched the beauty of Lake Erie to his left side. The sky was dressed in different colors as the sun completed his cycle for the day. Nature was still beautiful, unaware of the troubles caused by human nature, John thought to himself as he walked. The wind was chilly, but not the worst for the season; it was a mildly cold evening in Buffalo.

Another figure waited on a bench along Canalside with two coffees. The man was shorter than John and huskier. He had a very full beard with mixed gray here and there. He spoke English with a very heavy Muslim accent. But he was very calm, polite and radiated an aura of intelligence that could only be acquired with many years of education and respect for himself, as well as others.

"John, *as salamu aleiykum*, my friend; I took the liberty of getting you a cup of coffee." Aqdas smiled at John as they shook hands. John sat by Aqdas, both radiating a peace that few people in life have experienced.

"Thank you, my friend," John answered as he opened the seal of his coffee- top to take a sip.

John looked at Aqdas and asked, "How do you feel?"

"*Ya ni,*" Aqdas answered, "So-so. You get old, *ya ni* is the best you can do." Aqdas answered very peacefully and he spoke with a smile that came from his soul and made his eyes shine.

"I wish I could say the same for the world," John said as he looked around."

"John, you know that the world has always been the same. The setting is always the same. The characters change because we are mortal. But the stories repeat themselves over and over again." Aqdas replied.

"The weapons have changed. They have become more powerful; more dangerous." John stated.

"Yes, they have become more advanced and sophisticated," Aqdas stated.

"Nothing sophisticated about killing people," John answered as he sipped his coffee.

Aqdas chuckled at John's statement, "Very true, my friend."

"Christians don't change; Hebrews don't change; Muslims don't change. The world has more ideals than truth and that has always been the same; that has always been a problem." John explained.

"Muslims," Aqdas smiled, "my people will never change. The violence began back in 632."

"When Muhammad died," John completed the thought for Aqdas.

"Correct. His followers couldn't decide if to follow a bloodline or a leader close to Mohammad; someone truly trained in the faith by Mohammad." Aqdas continued.

John deep in thought stated, "The Sunnis chose Abu Bakr. I believe he was Muhammad's advisor, first successor or Caliph, to lead the Muslim state."

Aqdas continued, "But the Shiites had a different opinion and they favored Ali."

John interrupted, "Yes, I believe he was Muhammad's cousin."

"And son-in-law." Aqdas added.

"Oh, ok. I wasn't sure about that part." John said with a smile.

"Ali and his successors are called imams, who do not only lead the Shiites but are considered to be descendants of Muhammad." Aqdas spoke as he enjoyed his coffee.

As the two friends spoke in their peaceful surroundings, many miles away in Syria, a group of Sunnis surrounded a known Shiite. The Shiite was on the floor, as the group of Sunnis kept him down, kicking him on the face, stomach and private parts. The Shiite tried to cover himself, but he was blacking out from all the hitting. The Sunnis kicked him until he couldn't move anymore as he lay on his stomach. The group of

Sunnis watched the man as he bled and a couple of them took out their cell phones to record everything. Others were yelling, chanting and cheering. Then one of the Sunnis wearing a black turbine covering his head and part of his face put one foot on the man's back, grabbed his hair and with a knife started to cut around the man's neck, as if he was a piece of meat and not a human being. He continued to cut until he reached the bone and then with great strength, he began to cut through the neck bone. The blood gushed everywhere. The man pulled and cut until the head was completely decapitated and separated from the body. Everyone continued in approval yelling and chanting around the body; as the head was carried off, by the hair as a trophy. The video of the incident was all over the news.

Back in Buffalo, New York the beautiful colors of the sunset were all over Lake Erie, as the two friends continued their conversation. John looked out at Lake Erie as he stated, "So much blood. So much hate. Sometimes it seems beyond repair. The human being is capable of loving so much, and yet, he is so very capable of also hating with such vigor, that he loses himself in the process."

Aqdas continued, "It actually gets deeper and more resentful."

John realized that Aqdas needed to speak about this. He realized that his friend was very distressed about his people and that there was something deeper in his heart that he had not shared yet. But he also knew his friend would not say anything until he was ready and it made no sense in trying to pull it out of him.

Aqdas continued, "Shia was originally a movement, not a people."

John thought about it, "That's right. They were actually referred to as Shiat Ali."

"Correct," Aqdas continued, "Which means, "Party of Ali". The Shiites followed Ali with great passion. They felt pride that Ali was a bloodline of Mohammad. Do you remember what happened in 661?"

"In 661 Ali was assassinated by the Sunnis." John answered.

"Correct. But also, Ali's both sons, Hassan and Hussein were denied their right to Caliphate or to become leaders." Aqdas explained.

"True," John stated as he reached deeply into his memory, "Hassan was poisoned in Muawijah in 680, who was actually the first Caliph of the Sunni Umayyad Dynasty."

Aqdas interrupted, "And Hussein was killed in the battle-field by Ummayads in 681. This bloodshed was unforgivable and the war between Sunnis and Shiites escalated." John and Aqdas drank their coffees' quietly as they rested deep in thought looking at the horizon.

Miles away in Iraq a Shia militia walked into a village of Sunni civilians. As the Sunnis began to run and hide, the Shia militia opened fire. Men, women and children ran for cover to save their lives. You could smell the burnt gun powder in the air as smoke was everywhere. Sunni Muslims of all ages were lying dead all over the streets. The bodies, the roads and the walls of the houses were all bathed with blood.

Back in Buffalo, New York John and Aqdas continued their conversation, as they sat in the Canalside overlooking Lake Erie. The air was crisp and by now the coffees were cold.

"Now, there is one important historical point that must be mentioned to complete the circle of the story." Aqdas was very animate about the conversation; for some reason he needed to continue with the story, as if by going back and forth with John he would discover something that he had never thought about before; a reason, a truth, an explanation for all the bloodshed of his people.

"After the 11th Imam died in 874, he left behind a young son that was very intelligent and admired by all." Aqdas continued, "Even though, he was very young he was already seen as a future leader of the Shiites."

John interrupted, "I remember reading about that. At his father's funeral the young boy disappeared. The Shiites saw the boy as a messiah who has been hidden from the public by God."

Aqdas continued, "The largest Sect of the Shiites, known as the 'Twelvers' has been preparing for his return."

"Yes, I remember reading about the Twelvers." John said deep in thought, "But *not* all Shiites were Twelvers."

"No," Aqdas continued, "The Shiites were divided into three groups: the Zaidis, the Ismailis and the Ithna-Asharis known as the Twelvers. The Twelvers, which is the largest group, believe that Muhammad's religious leadership, spiritual authority and divine guidance was passed to twelve of his descendants; beginning with Ali, Hassan and Hussein."

Then John said slowly as he followed Aqdas thinking, "That's why it was impossible for the Shiites to follow Muhammad's chief advisor Abu Bakr, like the Sunnis did."

"And," Aqdas continued, "That is why there was so much hatred after Ali and his sons were killed."

"Wow," John expressed a sense of disbelief, "It sounds like a Grim Fairytale."

"It is history, my friend," Aqdas said emphatically.

"So, now they wait for The Mahdi." John stated.

"Yes and the Mahdi will restore order," Aqdas explained.

"But will also destroy Christians and Jews." John added.

"No, no. He will allow the Christians and the Jews to convert to Muslim." Aqdas explained.

"Yeah...but if they don't convert...he will kill them." John stated; Aqdas nodded.

"Do you feel that The Mahdi will give the Christians and the Jews a chance to convert, while hoping in his heart that they don't convert in order to kill them?"

Aqdas smiled, "Who am I to talk about the heart of The Mahdi? Only The Mahdi can know his own heart. The Mahdi will come with love for those who worship Allah properly and death for those who don't. But everyone will be given a chance to find The Truth."

John looked away at the horizon. He knew his friend Aqdas was a very intelligent man.

"Love and Truth? Aqdas there has been a lot of bloodshed to be talking about love and The Truth. At some point after so much blood the ideals and the reasons get washed away. Aqdas you don't feel that if you participate in the faith of these Muslims that you carry in your soul the death of those killed by Muslims for not converting?" John stated looking at his friend.

"John, please," Aqdas smiled into John's eyes, "Could Christians cast the first stone? Have we forgotten Christian history? Can Christians judge Muslims? Have not the Christians filled their hands with blood of those who have not accepted their savior Jesus Christ? Let's talk about the Dark Ages, Christian atrocities committed towards people *believed, not proven* that were involved in witch craft or black magic,

THE TIME HAS COME

Catholic Church Inquisition, The Crusaders, The Conquista-
dores; bottom line, victims of the Christian Faith."

"A lot has gone wrong in the last two-thousand years and
people have turned the Christian Faith into another religious
doctrine. Christ died for the sins of the faithful Christian; but
some misguided Christians have killed Christianity. People
have always confused religion with faith. They do not mean
the same thing. True Christianity is faith and love." John
spoke with sadness in his face.

"And *true* Islam is faith, respect and love." Aqdas argued.
"Tell me John, do you feel that if you are a Christian, that you
don't carry in your soul the atrocities and bloodshed caused
by other Christians that have your faith and your Christian
teachings?" Aqdas argued.

Both friends stood quiet looking over Lake Erie.

*In the city of Mosul a big group of ISIS has waited for a
group of Christians; men, women and children to unite to read
the Bible and pray. The group of ISIS waited for about one-
hundred Christians to get on their knees, close their eyes and
bow their heads to pray. The large group of ISIS ransacked the
church shooting Christians, slicing heads and stabbing Christians. In a matter of a few minutes the massacre was completed
and the church was bathed in blood with the bodies of close to
one-hundred Christian Martyrs.*

"Aqdas," John asked, "It doesn't scare you that there is
very little difference between the Anti-Christ and The Mahdi
that the Muslims await for?"

"My friend," Aqdas smiled, "The Anti-Christ is coming to
destroy the Christians. The Mahdi is coming to give them an
opportunity to turn to Allah and correct themselves. The Anti-
Christ is coming to kill; while The Mahdi is offering salvation."
Aqdas answered.

"Salvation or death," John confirmed.

"A chance nonetheless," Aqdas answered.

"What about ISIS?" John asked.

"What about them?" Aqdas replied.

"Are they acting according to the teachings of Mohammad?"

"Oh, please, John," Aqdas laughed, "ISIS is nothing more
than the outcome of the United States unfinished business. At
the end of the Gulf War in March of 1991, after the United

States invaded Iraq and killed President Saddam Hussein, Saddam Hussein's militia group stuck together. During Saddam's thirty year reign, he murdered 150,000 Shiites. The United States were supposed to stay behind and kill the rest of the Sunni military group that Saddam left behind. Instead the American Soldiers were called back home."

"No, you are very wrong to say that, because you have to think about the purpose of the American Soldiers involved in the war. The purpose was to kill Saddam Hussein; which they did. The purpose was not to get involved in a war in the Middle East that is never going to end. Americans do not have a desire to kill or desecrate its youth. Americans do not worship God by sacrificing their young with the false illusion that God will bless them and their families if they die for God. Men have to go to war with the purpose of protecting its country and families once we have done that, it's time to go home. The Shiites and the Sunnis both are at war forever." John spoke emphatically.

"Okay, but the US has the illusion that war is like a chess game; that is not truth. The US many times has tried to kill a military leader, like when you play chess and you capture the King; game is over. But reality is not like that. Sometimes when you kill a leader, like in the case of Saddam Hussein; a trained army like ISIS, Iraqi branch of al-Qaeda, is left behind and continue the work of the dead leader. The Americans left the way for the Iraqi Shia Prime Minister with the power to destroy all Sunnis and ISIS have been fighting back. Understand, the American soldiers maybe had the right to go home; their war was over, but it was not over for the group that came to be known as ISIS."

"And it will never be over." John confirmed, "It's ridiculous. How long were those young American soldiers supposed to stay in Iraq fighting an endless war? ISIS was going to happen sooner or later, because war is the purpose of their lives. They are fanatical and they live, eat and sleep war. By 2003 Iran's Quds Force was financing both Shiites and Sunnis to kill Americans. What purpose did the American soldiers have to stay and help the Shiites when the Shiites themselves wanted to kill the American soldiers? The Shiites only wanted the help of the American soldiers to kill Saddam Hussein. Hypocrisy!"

They both sat quiet for a while.

John broke the silence, "My friend, what is going on with your health?"

"Nothing," Aqdas insisted.

"I could tell that you are sick," John declared.

Aqdas smiled, "You are always so shrewd. All right, last year I had a heart attack and I have a pace-maker. The doctors tell me that if I have another heart attack, it may be my last."

John looked at Aqdas in silence.

"How do you feel?" John asked.

"I feel fine. I look at this way; it would be silly that after spending my life looking for Allah, that I may get sad when I get the opportunity to see him. That would make me a hypocrite." Aqdas laughed.

John smiled.

Both men got up to leave; they shook hands and embraced.

"Good-bye, my friend." John said.

"Until next time." Aqdas smiled.

As Aqdas turned to leave, John stopped him, "Aqdas, what would you say to Jehovah, if you go before him and find out that the Christians were right?"

Aqdas smiled, "I would thank him for allowing me to be your friend all these years and blessing me, even though, I was wrong. And I would tell him that in my book you are the best servant his ever had. What about you, John? What would you say to Allah, when you die and find out that the Muslims were right?"

John smiled, "I would tell Allah, that my best friend Aqdas, is the best Christian I have ever met."

They both laughed and went their separate ways.

CHAPTER THIRTEEN

Power

The shiny black limousine rode through East Superior Street on a clear Chicago evening and stopped at one of the top hotels in the city. The limousine was guided by a black sedan with four Secret Service men and a patrol car with two of Chicago's best officers. Behind the limousine was another black sedan with four other Secret Service men. As the cars stopped on East Superior Street in front of the hotel the patrol car went ahead and crossed itself on Superior Street so no cars could pass. The black sedan stopped a few car lengths behind the limousine so that no cars behind them could get close to the limousine. Both Chicago officers got out of the patrol car and stood with their hand on their weapons looking around and signaling traffic to stop. The first black sedan's doors open and three Secret Service men jumped out and positioned themselves on the street and in front of the hotel. The second sedan behind the limousine opened the doors and three more Secret Service men jumped out and position themselves. One of the Secret Service men as he looked around walked to the backdoor of the limousine and opened the door. He held his hand out and the First Lady took his hand and stepped out of the limousine. A few people walking by were now beginning to hang around trying to take a peek at who was in the limousine. The secret agents and the officers were holding the people back. The President did not want his trip to Chicago to be announced. The people began to cheer and yell when they recognized the First Lady. She in return began to smile and wave. People with their phones began to take pictures and videos of the first lady.

After the First Lady the President of the United States stepped out of the limousine and as he straightened his body up a bullet struck his head. His scalp burst as blood and pieces of his skull and skin were spread throughout the limousine, sidewalk and the First Lady's dress and face. The First Lady screamed and instinctively moved to grab her husband; but was blocked off by a Secret Service man who threw his body on top of hers and pushed her back in the limousine to protect her. Another Secret Service man moved quickly to grab the body of the dead President before it hit the ground.

The shooter was a professional who knew he had not a second to spare. He waited patiently in the building across the street and when he saw the limousine of the President arrive with a steady hand he watched through his scope. The second the scope line up with the view of the President's head he slowly press the trigger without moving another part of his body. The shot was masterful and perfect as he watched through his scope the head of the President burst open. As the Secret Service men scrambled to take the President to a hospital and the First Lady to safety, the shooter very calmly put the weapon down on the floor, knowing very soon it will be found and walked down the stairs and out of the building the back way, very calmly and unnoticed. Before they arrived to the hospital The President of the United States was pronounced dead.

One hour later the cameras were on Vice-President George Paraish as he was being sworn to become President of the United States. Everyone listened as President Paraish gave his speech.

"My fellow Americans, I stand before you with a heavy heart; for we have lost a great President, but I also lost a great friend. I will not try to fill his shoes, for I do not know if I could be a great leader as he was. But I do understand that this great nation of ours has gone through some very difficult turmoil in a very short time. We have faced terrorism, natural disasters, civil movements, economic upheaval, the assassination of a president and treason; but I assure you that this is nothing in comparison with the strength of this country and what we are capable of achieving. The steps to correcting this country and bring it back to order begins now. I am President of the United States. The Martial Law in this country placed by our last President and Congress will continue indefinitely; as long as I see fit for the best of this country. Every military service men and women will be posted throughout the country ready to enforce Martial Law and anyone found not cooperating with the law will be treated as treason. This is the greatest country in the world and we will get back on our feet and stand firm in the eyes of the rest of the world and in history. Thank you."

As the President walked away from the reporters they tried to grab his attention to ask questions, President Paraish turned, raised his hand and said emphatically, "No questions!" President Paraish wasted no time in showing the reporters and the people in the nation that *he* was in charge.

"Sir," Jenna spoke to the President, "that was not the speech we prepared for you! We cannot put our effort and energy to create what would be the perfect speech for you and then you totally ignore the whole speech. With due respect Sir; I feel that you should have at least informed us that you were not going to use the speech."

The President stopped walking and looked at Jenna squared in the eyes, with a straight serious look. Jenna has never felt so belittled just by a look.

"Jenna," the President said calmly, "where is your partner Frank?"

"I am here, sir." Frank was standing by the side.

"Good I am glad you are both here. I hate to do things twice. You are both fired. These two agents will escort you to your offices and one hour from now escort you out of the building. Use you hour diligently or your things will stay behind." The President turned his back them and walked away.

Half hour later the phone rang and President Paraish said, "Hello."

"Good-evening, President," The Voice said with a smile.

"Good-evening," The President replied.

"How do you feel?" The Voice asked.

"Like a new man." The President replied.

"Excellent. You have done well for yourself and your family. I can see that great things will come your way. We have both kept our part of the agreement. Now we must continue to work together." The Voice assured.

"Yes, I agree." The President reaffirmed.

"Mr. President," The Voice continued, "Get in touch with Prime Minister Taylor and explain to him how as the new leader of the United States you want to join Europe and their venture into the future of Micro-chips. The Micro-chip will be your key to controlling your nation. They are going forward with the distribution this week and it is the perfect time for you to join them. The United States will be a great renovated Nation, with a new President and "Big Brother" watching and controlling every move that everyone makes. You will be known as the President that stopped terrorism in the United States and everyone will love you for that."

"That sounds very good to me; real power." The President stated.

"More power than you have ever imagined." The Voice exclaimed.

"Just remember Mr. President," the Voice said calmly with a smile, "I made you. You are my project and I can destroy you. Enjoy your power. But do not forget the roots of your power or your fruits will rotten. Understood?"

"Yes...Sir." The President said understanding.

"Good. Now get in touch with Prime Minister Taylor." The Voice hung up.

President Paraish sat in his office hearing the dial-tone. That was the first time that President Paraish hung-up the phone with The Voice and felt fear. Before everything seemed good; as if finally he could feel true power. Paraish knew that he could never be President, unless he was a Vice-President and the door was opened through an assassination. America is funny the process of choosing their President is so long and yet, the Vice-President is basically nominated by the President, with some input from the cabinet; but if the President gets killed, who really chose this new person about to become President; surely, not the people. It seemed like a far-fetched plan, but The Voice told him it would work...and it did. The President is dead, he is President but Paraish couldn't help feeling in the pit of his stomach a knot, a fear, that The Voice was too good at controlling the situation; any situation. Paraish kept in mind that he was part of an organization, a Secret Society that was more powerful than any anyone could imagine. He was President of the United States and a member of the illuminated minds of the most powerful Secret Society in the world. This was a power that Congress had never experienced."

He pressed the speakerphone, "Get me the Secretary of Defense Carl Eisenhower."

"Yes, Sir." The secretary jumped.

Less than ten minutes later the Secretary of Defense was knocking at the door.

"Mr. President, you call, Sir?" The Secretary of Defense asked.

"Carl, sit down. Relax. You and I will be working very close in putting this country back in shape."

"Okay, Sir." The Secretary of Defense was responded eagerly.

"What would you say are the major problems we are facing in this country?" President Paraish asked.

"Well, Sir," The Secretary of Defense started, "We have the south with its different movements whether they are racial or trying to separate from the Union."

"I understand. Remember I am from the south. I will handle that problem personally." The President acknowledged.

The Secretary of Defense nodded, "Okay. Then we have the center, they are trying to survive and their cities are practically demolished."

"Okay. Continue." The President demanded.

"The west is basically under water and up north they have become "separatist"; they have not verbalized it like the south but it's an area of lots of mountains and they shoot first and ask questions later. From the south-east up to the north-east they are flooded and could use all the help they can get. That's about it, Sir. The people are upset, Sir. This is much worse than Katrina many years ago and people remember how long it took for the government to help their own nation. They will not tolerate this time and are fighting back."

"This will not be another Katrina and these people will get proper help, timely and they will also not turn this country upside down. If they try to create chaos they will find themselves on the wrong side of the law.

There was a knock on the door. The President yelled, "Come in."

A few gentlemen walked into the room and the President got up rubbing his hands and full of energy. He extended his hands to them and shaking them. "Welcome, gentleman. Please sit down. We have here Secretary of Defense Carl Eisenhower, Vice-President Ron Fletcher, and Floor Leader of the Senate Harold Reins, Republican Senate Leader Ritch McDonald and Democratic Senate Leader Barry Sanders. Gentleman I have brought us together, because together we will bring this country back in order. Every state will continue to have American Soldiers implementing and enforcing Martial Law. We will not tolerate any form of anti-American movement verbal or physical. People will be controlled peacefully or aggressively; it depends on them. If they retaliate with aggression our boys will have the green light to defend themselves and the safety of our citizens. Understood? I want every military movement outside of the country closed and I want every American soldier back home."

"Sir, what about Israel? We always have military bases in Israel" Harold Reins asked.

"What about Cuba? Guantanamo?" Barry Sanders asked.

"If you men feel strong about having certain amount of men in designated areas throughout the world, then agree on a list and have it my office right away. But understand for the security and stability of this country, I want the Martial Law implemented stronger than ever and most of the American soldiers here on our land." The President spoke seriously and looking at everyone in the room as they all agreed with him. The President was pleased that everyone was cooperative, but he couldn't help wonder if The Voice was behind this mysterious cooperation. He told the President who to include in the meeting and in his plan. How did The Voice know it would go so smooth?

After the meeting the President sat at his office looking over some papers when his secretary rang, "Yes?" The President answered.

"Sir, I have bad news." The Secretary started.

"Yes?" The President waited.

"It's Karl Garret, Sir. He was found in his office with a shot in his head. He was found dead with the gun in his hand." The secretary spoke with a lump in her throat.

The President was silent. "Thank you, Eleonore. Make sure we send the family our respects."

As the President hung-up, he smiled.

As the President of the United States sat alone in the dim light of his office, picked up the phone and dialed slowly. The phone rang on the other side.

"Hello," Said the voice with the English accent.

"Prime Minister Taylor, it is the President of the United States. How are you?"

"I am doing well, thank you."

"We need to speak." The President continued.

"Yes. Indeed we need to speak."

CHAPTER FOURTEEN

The Night of a New Era

The hall at Buckingham Palace was bright, full of life and dressed for "The Night of a New Era". So read the signs outside and the screens inside the hall were all the tables were dressed with the most expensive linen white and red table clothes, porcelain, crystals and silverware. Everyone could feel the energy in the room as different rulers and representatives of European countries and allies around the world were all gathered together in peace and friendship towards one goal. The leaders of Europe were gathered together to introduce the "New European Union" and the induction of the human "Micro-Bio Chip" into the European and the American way of life.

Ahead of the spectacular evening was Prime Minister Taylor, as he was introduced as the leader of the "New European Movement" and "The Head" of the induction of the circulation of the human "Micro-Bio Chip" throughout Europe and The United States. Everyone stopped to eat and drink to applaud. Prime Minister Taylor walked slowly and with elegance; as he savored the moment. Knowing that at this instant he sealed not only his moment in England's history, but of the world also. He had just become a part of history and the future at the same time. The Prime Minister knew how to enjoy the moment and make it last as he walked slowly and stood behind the podium. The cameras were flashing; applause was loud and the excitement began to unwind as Prime Minister Taylor stood ready to speak.

"Ladies and Gentleman, welcome everyone to a historical night." Everyone applauded as the Prime Minister completed his sentence and looked around. "Tonight is the beginning of a new era. Where countries from Europe which go back thousands of years in history join today's technology and will lead tomorrow in a new way of life through the Micro-bio Chip. This chip is an incredible Enovation that it is not only going to unite most countries in Europe, but it is going to unite Europe with the United States across the ocean. At this moment I like to introduce the new President of the United States, President George Paraish." Everyone applauded as the President of the United States got up, waved and smiled.

The Prime Minister continued, "We have an ensemble of world leaders President Dubois, President Fischer, President Barbo." Everyone applauded after each name. "President Adamik, President Byrne, Prime Minister Elizabeth Stensby, Prime Minister Thorngren, and President Saarela. Ladies and gentlemen, I present to you the leaders of Europe!" Everyone continued to applaud. This was a great moment in history and Prime Minister Taylor looked around with pride as he stood in the middle of the great extravaganza as a leader. The lights, applause, and flashes it was more than any one leader of a country could ever dream to achieve. More than he ever imagined for himself.

Prime Minister Taylor raised his hand and everyone began to settle down. The Prime Minister continued his speech, "First, I like to announce that every leader in this room has already implanted a Micro-Biochip and we are ready for the future. Please raise your hands!" As Prime Minister Taylor yelled these words out every leader in the room raised there right hand and they all had Biochips implanted in their hands. Everyone applauded as Prime Minister Taylor took control of the room again and continued to speak.

"Thank you. Thank you. We have taken a big step today. We all have the Micro-Biochip implanted. I also have two big announcements to make to everyone here tonight. First, we are prepared to, right here tonight, to implant the Micro-Biochip in anyone that is here tonight."

Everyone started to applaud.

"And become part of the future by the time you leave here tonight." Prime Minister Taylor looked around; everyone applauded. "On screen #1, as you can tell our screens are numbered, you will see a number. When you see the number of your table, which is the number on the beautiful floral centerpiece, everyone sitting at the table may go to those curtains to the side and behind the curtains you will find people ready to implant your Micro-Biochip, which will be with you for the rest of your life. Welcome to the future. Any questions may be directed to the people doing the implants. These people have been educated in being able to explain any concerns you may have. Please if for any reason, which is beyond my comprehension, anyone does not wish to get the Micro-Biochip tonight, please don't worry. Go to the back anyway, ask questions and take the opportunity to educate yourself about the Micro-Biochip and we would also let you know what number to call once you are ready to join us."

Everyone applauded as Prime Minister Taylor looked around.

"There is one more announcement that I have to make." Prime Minister Taylor continued. "We have prepared and separated 1,000,000 Micro-Biochips for each leader in this room. These Chips will be travelling back to their countries in order for them to start distributing the Chips throughout their country." Everyone applauded. "My friends, the future is here!" The room roared with applauds and cheers. Prime Minister Taylor was on top of the world and everyone was standing and applauding.

As the applause subsided Prime Minister Taylor had to do one more thing that he did not want to do, but he had no choice. "Ladies and gentleman, now it is with great honor that I invite President Fischer from Germany to come and join me at the podium, so that he may inform us and show us the progression of the new Intelligent Service of Europe."

Everyone was a little astonished at this announcement. They applauded with respect, but everyone was more inquisitive than excited. President Fischer walked slowly to the podium, applauds continued. President Fischer and Prime Minister Taylor shook hands, as the flashes caught the moment and everyone applauded with a little more of enthusiasm. People were not quite sure what to expect; it had definitely become a night of surprises.

President Fischer took over the microphone, "Thank you, Prime Minister Taylor and thank you all for that welcome." Prime Minister Taylor stepped back and sat down.

President Fischer stood very erect, his small glasses at the point of his nose as he spoke. "Europe is definitely changing. We are definitely stepping into the future, like Prime Minister

Taylor has pointed out. But are we safe? Is Europe free from the shadows lurking over us described as Terrorists? Can we unite and enjoy the fruits of our changes, our technological advancements, our new world when we know that at any moment an act of terrorism may bring our joy to a halt and constantly live with fear of the dreadful shadow lurking over us. We must not live in fear! And definitely, we must not ignore that which is creating the fear.

Terrorism is the cancer of society. It is taking away lives, our peace of mind and the right that we have to enjoy our lives, without worry that somewhere a car at any moment may blow-up. We have the right to live without fear.

The Human Micro-Biochip will be placed in the hands of every European citizen and every American Citizen. This means that everyone wearing the Chip will be located and identified in a matter of seconds from headquarters through our computers at Central Intelligence. The communication between the European countries and with the United States will be measured in seconds. This mean God forbid if there is an adult missing, a child missing or abducted, a prisoner escaped or someone walking free, but suspected of any crime or terrorism could be found and arrested in a matter of minutes." Everyone applauded, as they realized the positive message that President Fischer was transmitting; but you could also feel that a lot of people in the room had questions and mixed feelings about this innovation. President Fischer was a very intelligent man and as he looked around he could feel that there were some people that feel reluctant to the news.

"Ladies and gentleman, I know that you are asking yourself if we are not putting a high price on our safety. It sounds like we are sacrificing freedom for safety. But I ask you, what price do you put on the safety of your family, your spouse, or your children? No one will constantly be checking to see who is where and what they are doing. The chips will be used by the officers in order to resolve some form of crime by finding the culprit or culprits. Reporters or a paparazzo will not have access to the system to find a person. The computers will be controlled by agents of the organization. Those of us and everyone in this room who are law abiding people will have everything to gain and nothing to lose. I am here to talk about the safety of Europe only, not the benefits that the chip will bring on the daily use. But I know that there will be no need for cash, credit or debit cards. There will be no need for house keys or car keys. Our medical records, our insurance information on and on will all be literally on our hands ready to use at any moment. But more importantly, you are the beginning of the future. The people in this room will be known as the 'Genesis' of the world to come." Now everyone applauded with more enthusiasm.

President Fischer continued, as Prime Minister Taylor watched him with amazement. President Fischer *is* doing a good job manipulating these people; too good of a job. Prime Minister Taylor looked at President Fischer convinced that The Voice was speaking and guiding him. He wondered if The Voice had President Fischer blackmailed. Was President Fischer living in fear of The Voice doing as he commanded? Or did they have a different form of relationship, one of mutual respect? Prime Minister Taylor knew that he would probably never be able to answer these questions. But he knew he could never like or trust President Fischer.

President Fischer continued, "Now if we may dim the lights and look at the screen behind me. Ladies and gentleman I introduce you to ISE-Intelligent Service of Europe." The room got darker, the screen went on and the German Lieutenant-General Schaeffer came on the screen, "Hello, I am Lieutenant-General Schaeffer. Welcome to this portion of the evening. I will have the pleasure of giving you a brief summary of how the men of ISE or Intelligent Service of Europe are being prepared to serve Europe and combat Terrorism." As Lieutenant-General Schaeffer spoke on the screen there were agents training hard on a form of boot camp, hand to hand combat, sharp shooting, disassembling explosives and attending classes on the understanding of the thinking and behavior behind the mind of the terrorist. The agents were being trained in what to look for in public places in order to spot terrorist candidates and how to properly disable the situation without alarming or threatening innocent lives. President Fischer stood watching the film with pride, as Prime Minister Taylor watched in amazement. Everyone in the room was in awe. Lieutenant-General Schaeffer continued, "These men and women are the new safety of Europe that will combat terrorism and allow us to move around in Europe with peace of mind and freedom. These are 500 men or women from each country of Europe represented here tonight that will return to their country ready to be the main law of Europe and create law and protection throughout Europe. I introduce to you the first 4,500 agents of ISE." As Lieutenant-General Schaeffer spoke the screen changed to 4,500 agents dressed in black pants and coats, with red lines on the side of the pants and red shoulder flakes. The black shoes were perfectly shined. The gold shields on the left side of their chest representing ISE. It was a gold shield with the map of Europe, the letters ISE and a shield ID number all in gold. They all had on their Officers Hat with the same shield in the front of the hat over the black shiny visor as they all marched in perfect unison. On the left arm of the coat they had a map of the country they belonged to and the name of the country over the map. On the right arm they had lines and symbols to describe their ranks just like in any military organization. The men and women marched in perfect unison as President Fischer watched with pride and everyone in the room applauded with intensity. President Fischer signaled to someone to pass to him his glass of champaign and as he lifted his arm, so did everyone in the room as he yelled out, "To a new and safe Europe!" Everyone in the room yelled with agreement as they were caught up in the excitement of the moment and toasted with President Fischer; as Prime Minister Taylor stayed back in the shadows watching. President Fischer rapidly said, "Excuse me, one more thing. President Paraish, I like to welcome you from the United States. I was not aware of you joining us, but I am glad. If you wish to communicate with me in uniting ISE with American soldiers, it would be my pleasure."

The President of The United States smiled, "Thank you, Sir. We will have our own group ready, but The New European Union and The United States will definitely work together against terrorism." Everyone applauded.

"Yes, sir!" President Fischer agreed. "I will like to say one more thing. All the ISE Agents have Micro-Biochips implanted. They are truly a part of The New Europe and the future of the United States. Thank you." Everyone applauded with enthusiasm. President Fischer walked off the stage. Prime Minister Taylor came back on the microphone, "Thank you, President

THE TIME HAS COME

Fischer, for that presentation. Now ladies and gentleman, it is up to you whether you join our New Europe Union tonight or another day. As you eat and we enjoy our evening, please feel free to go behind the curtains to speak with the representatives or get the Micro-Biochip implant tonight. Thank you and enjoy your night." Everyone applauded and Prime Minister Taylor was charming as ever as he walked to his table. Everyone continued to eat and many people were vigilantly watching the screen as they waited to see their table number so they could go behind the curtains.

As the evening ended close to dawn and Prime Minister Taylor and his wife were home, the Prime Minister watched his wife go quickly into a sound sleep as he walked to his home office haunted by thoughts. He knew the night was a success, but for whom? He was not sure if the evening truly was the salvation of Europe. This was not feeling good or right anymore. He sat at his desk trying to shut his mind off. Push the thoughts away and empty his heart of all feelings. But he couldn't. He had gone too far. It was too late to go back or to say, I don't want to be part of this anymore. There are things you can't fix; you just have to face the consequences. Something was wrong, but he couldn't explain what it was or what he was feeling. The silence was ripped apart by the sound of the phone. Prime Minister Taylor knew who it was and he did not wanted to speak to him.

"Hello." Prime Minister Taylor answered the phone.

"Hello," returned The Voice with enthusiasm, "Don't tell me you are tired."

"Actually, I am very tired." Taylor spoke softly.

"This was the biggest night of all our efforts and it was a success. You should be rejoicing!" The Voice insisted. "We have done more with words and manipulation than empires have done with war. We have basically united a couple of continents without killing a single life or shooting a single bullet. Sir, you have reasons to be proud of yourself." The Voice laughed softly.

The Voice noticed no reaction from Prime Minister Taylor.

"Well, I have more good news for you," Prime Minister Taylor said reluctantly.

"What is it?" The Voice asked.

Prime Minister Taylor continued, "I got a call from Cardinal Scarpato today."

"You did?" The Voice listened.

"The Cardinal said, The Papal conclave, The Pope with his group of Cardinals convened and have agreed to accept the Micro-Biochip into the Vatican. He also expressed his knowledge of when the news of the Vatican is made public, the amount of Catholics throughout the world that are going to want to have the Micro-Biochip implanted in them because it is accepted by the Vatican. Therefore, The Vatican wants 10 per cent of every dollar made on incorporating a Catholic into the Micro Biochip business." Prime Minister Taylor concluded.

The Voice listened and started to laugh. Prime Minister Taylor waited quietly.

"Of course they want 10 per cent. I am actually amazed that they don't want more! This is indeed, a sweet day! We have The Vatican!"

"We will give them the 10 per cent?" Prime Minister Taylor asked.

"Without a doubt. That is nothing." The Voice answered.

"That is basically three times what we are giving any other country." Prime Minister Taylor added.

"Well, they are basically worth three times more than any other country. So, fair is not equal." The Voice answered. There was silence.

"Prime Minister Taylor, I want to thank you for your service. I want you to know that you have been a great deal of help to me and our plan."

Prime Minister Taylor listened to The Voice, not knowing what to say.

"I know you are not happy. What's wrong?" The Voice asked.

"I understand that you are trying to do something good for Europe. At least I think. Even though, I don't appreciate how you got me into this, I was caught up in the belief that everything is for the greater good. But I don't trust President Fischer and I don't appreciate the fact that you have gone behind my back, working out your plans with others and left me in the dark. Tonight was the peak of my career and yet, I feel as though it was the downfall of my humanity. I no longer feel right about what we are doing. I feel like I have sold my soul." Prime Minister Taylor was silent.

"I understand," The Voice continued, "you want out."

"Yes...I do," Prime Minister Taylor answered.

"Well, like I said, thank you for your services. We won't need you anymore."

Prime Minister Taylor was confused by these words.

"What do you mean?" The Prime Minister asked.

"Prime Minister, be a man. If you are a coward I will do it for you, but there is a price, your family. If you're man and you do it yourself, you will be saving your family." The Voice spoke slowly.

"You want me...to kill ...myself?" The Prime Minister asked with disbelief.

"You want out." The Voice continued, "This is the best way."

"Who you think you are? I am the Prime Minister of England. No one asks me to kill myself." The Prime Minister spoke with indignation.

"Oh, on the contrary, I have helped many and I have asked many for their soul in return and to kill themselves. Either you do it Prime Minister or I will do it to you and your family. Be a man." The Voice spoke softly.

"Who do you think you are?" The Prime Minister asked.

"Do you want to know who I am?" The Voice asked.

"Who the hell are you?" The Prime Minister yelled as the first sounds of birds chirping in the early dawn came from outside.

"I will tell you who I am. Revelation 13, my friend. You will know who I am. Good-bye, Mr. Taylor." The Voice hung up.

Prime Minister Taylor sat on his chair listening to the dial tone of the phone. His body felt numb with fear. He slowly walked to his bookshelf and grabbed the old family Bible given to him by his grandfather. The Bible had been in the family for generations and he does not remember the last time it was open. He blew the dust away and opened to the book of Revelation. He searched for chapter 13 and as he read to himself, his eyes opened wide. "My God, could it be?"

Regardless, if it was true or not; he knew his family would be dead if he did not act like a "man". He walked to his desk, opened the draw at the bottom and found the old 38 sitting there. Took the box of bullets and put one in each cylinder. Took a bottle of bourbon and began to drink his last breakfast. When his body and mind were numb enough, he brought the gun to his head and pulled the trigger. Prime Minister Taylor was dead, but his family was safe.

CHAPTER FIFTEEN

Chaotic Harmony

John opened the heavy wooden doors of the little steeple church in Buffalo, NY and quietly stood and observed the environment. There were three Brazilian men, hired by Pastor Silva, drilling, using an electric saw and hammering creating noise and dust everywhere. It was a hot sunny day and you could see the air full of dust in the sun rays coming in through the church windows. John stood their thinking to himself that sometimes you need to destroy, create chaos, and modify to renew, create something new or even make it better. That is what God does with us sometimes, he allows our lives to become destroyed to bring us to our knees and then he renews our lives.

As John watched the men working Pastor Silva walked in from the back of the church. He smiled right away when he saw John.

"My brother, we have missed you so much. Where have you been?" The Pastor asked as he walked to John and shook his hands.

With the noise of the drill, the electric saw and the hammering it was difficult to hear each other. John made a sign to his ear as he shook his head and smiled. The Pastor made a sign towards the door to step outside. As the church door closed behind them they sat on the front steps of the church.

"God bless you, Pastor. How are you?" John asked.

"I am doing alright, my brother. But what happened to you? You have been gone for a week and I have been concerned about you, my friend."

John peacefully explained and smiled, "Thank you for worrying about me, I am not use to people worrying about me. I had to leave town to take care of some business." John did not wish to give the details of Aqdas' death or funeral.

"We are family and I will always worry about you. Is everything alright? Is there something I could do for you?" Pastor Silva asked with sincerity.

"No, thank you. I'm fine. How is the church?" John asked changing the subject.

"I finally put together the money to fix the damage from the earthquake, thank God. Some areas in the walls were badly damaged and the frames had some mild damage. They told me it was not so bad, but I want to make sure it's safe for the congregation. Also, I want to make sure it could withstand if, God forbid, another earthquake occurs."

"How long before the church is ready?" John asked.

"A week from this Sunday is my goal." The Pastor answered looking up at the sky and placing his hands together as if praying.

John nodded and looked around quietly as if in deep thought.

John turned to the Pastor again and asked in a serious, concerned voice, "Pastor, are you ready?"

The Pastor looked at John confused, "John, I just said, hopefully by a week from Sunday the church will be ready. I can't foresee returning any earlier."

"I know that everyman is born with a purpose and I am certain that our purpose has arrived. The time is here." John spoke almost absentmindedly.

The Pastor analyzed John very carefully. He had respect for John and he knew that John was a man of God, with great understanding of the word, but sometimes he spoke in riddles and it was difficult for him to agree or disagree.

"And what do you think is our purpose?" The Pastor asked.

"I find it very strange that Prime Minister Taylor committed suicide after the biggest night of his life. He worked so hard for the unification of Europe and on the night that his goal is sealed, he goes home and commits suicide. I would have understood if he was assassinated like our President, but suicide?"

"You believe that someone pressured Prime Minister Taylor into committing suicide?" Pastor Silva asked.

"Add to that, that the President of the United States was assassinated a week before." John continued speaking as if thinking out loud.

"The President gets assassinated and he wants nothing to do with the Human Micro Bio-chip. The Vice-President becomes President and he wants the Bio-chip for our country. A week after he is inaugurated he is in Europe to engage in the movement and the Prime Minister commits suicide."

"Do you think the incidents are connected?" Pastor Silva asked.

"Yeah, I do think that everything is connected." John answered.

The Pastor listened very attentively, "You make it sound as if there is someone or a group behind everything that is happening; a chaotic harmony of some kind." Pastor Silva observed.

"Europe is no longer the same. The European army or police that has been placed with members of the different countries in Europe have over-ridden the power of Interpol or the United Nations. The Biochip has become a way of life in Europe and the United States have become partners precisely at a time when conveniently we are under Martial Law and can't fight back without being treated as out-laws. It's chaotic harmony alright." John explained.

"There are rumors of Christian Churches closing and not being allowed to congregate." Pastor said.

"They are not rumors. A basic rule of Martial Law is not allowing groups to form in order for the people not to be able to form strength or plans against the government. We will not be able to congregate and the Bio-chip will be enforced upon us." John explained.

Pastor Silva added, "The Vatican has accepted the Bio-chip and the Pope has urged all Catholics around the world to participate. He said, how did he put it, The Biochip has brought most of Europe and the United States together, and soon it will bring the rest of the world together. He stated that it is his answer to World peace."

"The blind will lead the blind," John stated.

"I received my letter from the government, with the appointment for the Biochip." Pastor Silva said.

"I received my letter too. We must not under any circumstances give in to the request." John stated emphatically.

"John, there is a meeting of Christian Churches tomorrow night. Pastor Anderson from The First Methodist Church is heading the meeting and numerous churches are going to be there. He has a strong faith and is worried about all the Christians. He wants us to plan ahead to stick together and help one another in order to survive what he is referring to as "The first wave of Revelations."

"The time of Denominations and comfortable religion is coming to an end. Christianity was never supposed to be a religious order; it was supposed to be a way of life, a way of thinking. Religion destroyed the true purpose of Christianity and now we are going to have to go back to the days of the apostles, when they were persecuted by Rome, or we will have to resign our Christian belief. The only way we, as Christians, could survive this period in history is by uniting in faith in the name of Jesus, our Lord and Savior; giving up all the dogmas, rules and preference of our denomination. Faith, love and prayer in Jesus' name with the Word of God in our lips and engraved in our hearts." John spoke as if in a trance.

"The combining of the Christian churches will not be easy. Pride will get in the way." Pastor Silva added.

"Where there is pride, the Holy Spirit is not. That is why the Bible states, 'Many will be called, few will be chosen', because many are dead churches without the Holy Spirit and they will not survive the years of Satan's Rule." John answered.

Pastor Silver agreed, "Pride is destroying the south right now. After the earthquake they have posted themselves as separating from the Union. Many want nothing to do with Washington and they are fighting a second Civil War. They are stating that since we have Martial Law, that the laws protecting black people in the south no longer apply and have reinstated segregation. Thank God, the army is down there maintaining some order, but it's a war zone."

John listened attentively, "They wasted no time."

John continued, "The Anti-Christ, is the father of manipulating people and he will have one last chance to rule. The people that have not learned to have a sincere relationship with the Spirit of God will not be able to have spiritual strength or wisdom to fight his lies. The Anti-Christ will connect groups that consider themselves above the rest of the world either by their riches or their knowledge and either way it's just pride. Their pride will blind and kill them."

The Pastor asked, "You are convinced that this is the work of the Anti-Christ?"

At that moment the conversation was interrupted by the arrival of Michael.

"Hi," Michael spoke with a low voice.

Michael seemed preoccupied with something.

Pastor Silva asked, "Are you alright? You seem to be carrying a heavy burden."

John asked, "Michael, do you wish to speak to the Pastor alone?"

"No, it's ok. I might as well speak to both of you." Michael answered in a sheepish voice.

He continued, "Well, Debby is pregnant."

"That's great!" The Pastor yelled out. John was quietly watching Michael.

"Well, these aren't the best of times. We are worried. We wanted to have a baby, but with everything happening in the country is so sudden; with Martial Law and everything." Michael spoke nervously.

Pastor Silva looked at Michael with concern, "My God, you are not planning to abort the child?"

"What?" Michael asked, "No. No, it's not that."

"Then, what is it?" John asked.

"We received a letter from the government and if we do not do the Biochip implant we will not have medical care for Debby or the baby." Michael spoke with great sadness.

The Pastor's eyes opened wide as he spoke nervously, "Michael, think about what you're doing! Think of your family!"

"I am thinking about my family! That's the problem!" Michael threw back at the Pastor. John listened quietly.

"It's easy for John, no family. You Pastor, your kids are older; but a baby?" Michael explained with anguish.

"Michael, we are a church. We are family. We are having a meeting with other churches tomorrow night to try to figure out how we could all help one another and prepare for the situation. Please wait another day and come to the meeting and let's put our faith together and fight this in unison. You are not alone. Please let us help you both. Don't do this." The Pastor pleaded.

"Pastor, I don't want to do this. I will go to the meeting tomorrow. If we do not find a way to help Debby and the baby, I wash my hands. I do not feel responsible for what I have to do. But if it's God's will to find a solution, I hope it comes quickly." Michael spoke looking at the Pastor.

"It will, son. It will," The Pastor answered.

"Text me the information for tomorrow's meeting. Good night," Michael turned around and left.

Pastor Silva and John sat quietly at the steps analyzing what just happened.

Their hearts felt heavy and sad. They truly needed a miracle to help Michael and Deborah. As they sat their quietly an American soldier walked up to them.

"Is this the church of Pastor Silva?" The soldier asked without emotions.

"Yes it is and I am Pastor Silva." The Pastor answered.

The soldier continued, "Sir, this is a letter from the United States Government informing you that it is illegal for any group of any kind to congregate while the country is under Martial Law. Therefore, tomorrow at 8:00 am all churches as well as clubs or public halls will be chained and closed until further notice or the Martial Law is lifted. If you have any belongings in the building, make sure you take them out tonight."

"You are closing my church?" Pastor Silva asked with anger.

"Sir, if you have any questions you may call the number provided in the letter for you." The soldier said coldly.

"Good night." The soldier said as he turned around and walked away.

Pastor Silva stood at the steps of his church dumbfounded.

"My God, what is happening?" Pastor Silva yelled.

John broke his silence as he spoke slowly.

"Like I said before," Pastor Silva looked at him, "Pastor Silva, are you ready?"

CHAPTER SIXTEEN

Aliyah! The Land of Israel!

Yannel Schol arrived at Jerusalem early in the dawn. The first rays of the morning sun were breaking through the darkness as he reached the Western Wall where he prayed as a young man with his father. Everywhere he looked, he saw memories of his life that now seem much more like a distant dream. He looked at the wall and thought to himself, if the wall could echo the voice of his people you would hear the lamentations of the Jewish people throughout the centuries.

Yannel continued to walk through his old streets to his cousin's house. He wanted to see and speak with his cousin Alter before seeing his father. He remembered the last conversation with his father, when he informed his father that he has become a Christian and that he was going to the United States. His father did not look at him and with no emotions told him in Yiddish, "Don't be silly, tomorrow I expect you at the market. We have a lot of work to do," as he walked away. Yannel sat in his father's house waiting respectfully to finish the conversation. His father went to sleep. They never finished the conversation. Yannel went to the United States and ten years have passed.

Yannel walked the streets of Jerusalem until he reached his cousin's house. Everything seemed older and the streets seemed smaller. He had spoken to his cousin Alter, who was very happy to receive Yannel at his home. When Alter opened the door they both looked at each other and exchanged emotional "Shalom". Yannel sat down with Alter and his wife and two boys to have breakfast, as they spoke about the past and the future.

"Are you going to see your father?" Alter asked.

"Yes." Yannel answered quietly with sadness. "I want to wash up and rest a while. Then I will go see him. I am tired from the trip."

"You know, your father is old. He looks older than what he is. He has suffered much and he is not strong; be careful." Alter spoke looking at his cousin.

"I will be careful and respectful. But I have to see my father," Yannel replied.

"Then see him, you will." Replied Alter reassuringly.

A few hours later Yannel walked what seemed an eternal walk from Alter's house to his father's house. When he arrived everything looked the same. It was the house of his birth. He knocked at the door and an old woman opened the door. She looked at Yannel's face and her eyes opened wide as her hand covered her mouth as to keep her last breath of life in her.

"Shalom, hima," Yannel greeted his mother.

His mother was wordless and she embraced Yannel as she felt her eyes fill with tears as they both cried. An old man came out from the bedroom and stood in the middle of the room looking at his wife.

"What is happening," the gentle old man asked.

The mother looked at her husband and without a word, pushed the door back and signed Yannel to come into the house. Yannel slowly stepped in and looked at his father, as his father looked at him in shock. As the father's shock passed, his father's face turned hard and cold as he stood in silence.

Yannel walked as he kept his eyes on his father, "Father, I have come to see you."

The father did not respond.

"Father, I do not wish for us to be like this. I love you. I want us to speak again before it's too late." Yannel tried to reason.

"Are you coming home to stay? Did you renounce *that* religion?" The father asked without looking at him.

"I am not staying and I can never renounce my Lord and Savior Jesus Christ. You don't understand God called me to be a Christian." Yannel spoke softly.

"God, Yahveh is the true and only God; the God of Abraham, Isaac and Jacob; the God of Israel! Yahveh would never ask you to turn your back to your people. I will not speak to the dead. Respect me! Do not come back to this house!" Slowly his father walked out of the room. Yannel watched him with tears in his eyes.

He slowly turned around and walked to the door where his mom was waiting looking at the floor.

"I will write to you through my cousin Alter." Yannel said as he hugged his mother.

"You have dishonored your father's name, don't write to me." The mother said very firmly.

"I will write anyway, even if you don't answer." Yannel walked away and as he walked he felt that he lost a part of his heart and soul that he will never recuperate.

For the next three days Yannel stayed with his cousin and his family. His cousin was like a brother, his wife was very attentive and the children were very likable. He met with old friends from childhood, as well as adulthood. Yannel visited his old school and walked through the old streets where could swear that he would hear the echoes of past voices and conversations.

One day he walked slowly to the Western Wall or the "Wailing Wall" as it is known to many people. Even though, he is now a Christian, he couldn't help feeling small and insignificant in front of this "Holy Wall". He walked up to the Wall and put his hands on the cemented stones of the Wall. He felt the rough texture of the Wall and the sharp unevenness of the stones' on the skin of his hands. How many centuries? How many tears? How much blood had stained the Wall? He was taught that the presence of God himself was at the Wall. Even as a Christian, he believed that the presence of Jehovah was there, crying for his people, their suffering and their misunderstanding. The same way that a father never stops wailing for his children, the same way that his father will never stop suffering because of his absence, it is the same way that God will never stop crying for his children, his people, Israel.

"Jesus, help us all please." He said out loud with great emotion. A great feeling came over him that produced a great pain in his heart, and he realized at that moment that the Wall would not always stand. He realized that the Wall would one day be rubble and he wept. His people's suffering was not over.

It was around 5:00 am and Yannel was awakened from the noise outside. He heard people yelling, singing and crying as they feasted with jubilee. He listened and slowly he began to get out of bed. He heard Alter tap his door.

"Cousin, you must get up!" Alter spoke loudly.

"What is it?" Yannel asked.

"Come to watch the news. Israel, the land of Abraham, has been returned to us! The President has signed a "Peace Treaty" with Syria and other countries of the Middle East. Come hear the news."

Yannel sat with a wrinkled forehead. He thought he was dreaming, but he knew he was wide awake.

"What?" He asked himself as he grabbed his robe as he headed to the bedroom door. He found Alter and his wife in front of the television as he sat down and listened attentively to the reporter on the screen.

"In 1948 Israel became a nation. Only to find their land constantly bombarded by the Arab-Islamic nations that surrounds it. Israel has never known peace or the enjoyment of having their land. Only their faith has helped them to survive. Only their tenacity has helped them to rise above the situation. They have proven to have a solid faith as they have continued to worship their God, even when they are surrounded by their enemies: Syria, Jordan, Egypt, Iraq, Turkey and many other organizations that have sworn to remove them from the land that they swear Israel wrongfully owns. Through the years Israel has found itself defending their land from the PLO, FATAH, HAMAS and HEZBOLLAH groups that have terrorize Israel. It is nothing less than a miracle that has helped this nation of faith and ancient customs to survive.

Now after all the bloodshed and the years of humiliation the Arab-Islamic World, much to the surprise of everyone, has proposed a written Peace Treaty for both sides to sign. This has come after it has been announced that the Islamic World is no longer divided. Even though, we know very little, it seems that the long awaited "Calif" has arrived. The one that supposed to come and guide the Muslim nations in unison, has instead of destroying Israel, allow them to have the land and summoned all true Muslims to Syria where there will be some form of great modification of the Muslim world. It also has been announced that any group acting on their own under the Muslim faith, without the consent of the Unified Muslim World will be considered an enemy. The Unified Muslim World is set to prove its faith has always been one of faith and love. We do not know who this long awaited Calif is, but the man has changed the Middle East. Israel is free to enjoy their land and to build their temple, to finally have a home for their God."

"You hear, Cousin," Alter yelled at Yannel, "you picked a great time to come back to Israel!" Yannel looked at the television screen, at his cousin and his wife, at the people at the streets; everybody dancing, everybody celebrating, but he does not feel right. He remembered the feeling at the Western Wall; he remembered the Bible and something doesn't seem right.

Yannel took his phone and called Pastor Silva.

"Hello, my brother, how are you?" Pastor Silva spoke, excited to hear Yannel's voice.

"Pastor, have you heard about the big news in Israel?" Yannel asked.

"Yes, it must be a very exciting time to be there." The Pastor replied.

"Well there is a lot of excitement. But I don't feel it. My visit here has very mixed emotions. I love my people and I should feel happy for them, but I don't. Isn't there something in the Bible about what is supposed to happen when Israel get their land back and build a new temple?" Yannel asked.

"The news did not say anything about a new temple." Pastor Silva answered.

"Over here, they are speaking of starting a new temple right away. That they will be the generation to do it right and that the new house of God has to be built before anything." Yannel explained.

"My brother, I am concerned about your words. In Revelation 11:2, it speaks about how at the end of times, Israel would be able to build the third temple. It is a very significant time, because when they start building the temple that means that the Anti-Christ is in the world and he has begun to put his plan into action. They will spend the first three and half years of the Anti-Christ's reign building the temple and then a great massacre will come upon Israel. The Anti-Christ will then continue to rule the world for three and half years and have the temple as his throne."

"So, then whoever is behind the Peace Treaty, is the Anti-Christ. So the Anti-Christ is coming through the Muslims?" Yannel asked.

"It's not that easy. Remember the Muslims have been taught faith and love. But they also have been taught that the Christian World is a hypocrisy, which in many cases it is. They have been taught that we are the bad guys and that their God is real. They have been taught that if we do not except their real God, that we deserve to die. They have been conditioned to be Anti-Christians. Satan does not care how his Anti-Christ persona gets powerful, he only cares about Christians getting destroyed and keeping more people from becoming Christians. The world has always been a victim the Satan's plan. The Anti-Christ is here. Yannel?"

"Yes, Pastor?"

"Come home."

CHAPTER SEVENTEEN

The Valley of the Shadow of Death

Pastor Joseph Wilkinson had been a pastor for thirty years. He had a congregation in Scottsdale, Arizona of over 1,000 people which forced them to do three services on Saturday and three services on Sunday. This did not include the millions of Christians that followed him on his television program every Sunday. He was the president of two national Christian organizations and was respected by the Christian community from coast to coast. Pastor Joseph Wilkinson had written over twenty books on different subjects of the Bible and even though he had many people that dislike him, they honestly were never able to find any black spots in his career or life. Many considered him to be a true "Man of God" and not like many in the past that were "wolves dressed in sheep skin".

The tall thin white haired man, stood at the podium in this beautiful clear, breezy night in the middle of the desert of Yuma, Arizona. There were benches provided for 24,000 Christians to sit brought by Christian truck drivers from around the country. There was a quick stage built roughly out of cheap lumber and a podium to look over the people, so that everyone could see and hear the speaker. On the back part of the stage there was a wooden cross that stood tall and proud symbolizing the most significant part of the Christian faith, the crucifixion of Christ. It was basically an outdoor church that was thrown together quickly to bring Christians from all over the country to unite in faith to resolve the life threatening situation that they were facing. So many people in a church or an auditorium would not fit and to rent out a stadium will impact too much attention. They were aware of the fact that because of Martial Law, they are not permitted to congregate. Everyone here was breaking the law. Everyone was putting their life in danger, for their faith. The dessert was the only rational answer.

The speaker looked out onto the sea of people. There were Christians from every state in the country. On the stage there were pastors who were presidents of distinguished Christian organizations from Baptist, Pentecostal, Adventists and many other denominations. Every Christian Denomination was represented at this reunion in the in the middle of the dessert. Generators gave life to the sound system and lights surrounding the area. It was a true miracle of faith and desire that materialized this significant moment in history. Pastor Silva, John and the small congregation sat in the massive sea of believers.

Everyone was quiet as Pastor Joseph Wilkinson spoke, "There are approximately 150,000,000 Christians of different denominations in the United States. There are approximately 2.2 billion Christians in the world. That is a pretty big number, but not when you consider that there are 7.4 billion people in the world. We are outnumbered by 5.2 billion people and that is a lot of people. You also have to consider that not all of the 2.2 billion Christians in the world can or are willing to pick up an automatic weapon and go to war; while a big population of 7.4 billion people in the world, are going to look at us as outcasts; many of them willing to kill us. Needless to say, we have a problem."

There was a lot of talk and whispering that went on in the crowd. Pastor Wilkinson waited for silence.

"Please let me have your attention. We must remember that the Bible teaches us "that our struggle is not against flesh and blood, but against the rulers, against the authorities, against the powers of dark world and against the spiritual forces of evils in the heavenly realm." How do we fight this battle? Prayer, prayer and more prayer." The Pastor yelled out and everyone responded with loud amen, which sounded like thunder as they, in unison, glorified God.

"We cannot fight our war with guns or weapons of destruction. We can't go on to kill those that will hurt us, persecute us and kill us; even though they will come after us to hurt us."

"Why not?" A young man from the crowd yelled out.

Pastor Wilkinson looked at the crowd in the direction of the young man's voice and calmly answered, "Because it is not the will of God. The Anti-Christ is here on Earth. We must remember that God's will, must be accomplished. He has become very powerful and he knows how to manipulate the masses. He hates God, Jesus, The Holy Spirit and everything relating to the Holy Trinity including the Word of God. He hates us, God's people, the Christians. We could only fight back in two ways, with prayer and love. And maybe you have become so used to hearing that, you are immune to those words. But the truth is that if we do not care enough about each other, if we do not love each other enough to stick together to help one another, then our prayers will be in vain. For faith without love, is a faith in vain. We must unite in faith, love and prayer to be strong enough to fight the spiritual war against Satan."

People started to yell and clap as they yelled, "Jesus!"

"We cannot focus anymore on the religious part of our faith and the difference of our denominations. We have to focus on our common ground which is faith in the name of Jesus. From now on we cannot be Baptists, or Pentecostal, or Seventh Day Adventists, or Methodists, or Anglican or etc. etc. etc. NO! From now on we have to be Christians! And have faith in the name of Christ; for if we continue divided, all Christians will perish and we will have no one to blame, but ourselves. We took the purity of Christianity and turned it into religion and in the process suffocated the power of the Holy Spirit. We will be judged for our lack of love for one another. The power of our faith depends on the love we have for one another, for that is the will of God. The times are changing and we, God's People, have to change with the times."

People started to cheer, yell and applaud. Everyone started to praise God and the voices were heard as one heart in the dessert of Yuma, Arizona, under the stars.

On another part of the world, in Italy, it was a beautiful day at the Vatican. President Fischer with Prime Minister Harper Williams of England sat in the garden of the Vatican with Cardinal Scarpo.

They drank tea as they spoke to one another.

"I am pleased to meet you, Prime Minister Williams. I have heard many good things about you." The Cardinal smiled.

"I am very pleased to meet you, Cardinal. I have heard of the many great things you have done for the Vatican."

"Thank you. We do what we can." The Cardinal answered.

"Now," the Cardinal changing the conversation, "where are we in our business?"

"Well, actually very well. Thanks to the push from the Vatican, we have countries throughout Central and South America pushing for the distribution of the Bio-chip implants; Brazil, Argentina as well as Mexico and other countries in between. Of course the Vatican will receive its due percent." President Fischer explained.

"Yes and it is appreciated. Not that the money is the principle thing in mind, we truly feel that this will unite the world. There will be fewer adversaries, more peace and union in the world because of the Chip. It has slowly become an answer to our prayers." Cardinal Scarpo explained.

"I wish we could do something about the other Christians, they hold a different opinion about the matter than the Vatican." President Fischer stated.

"They love to carry on about the Chip being part of the number of the beast and the Anti-Christ. It's absurd!" Prime Minister Williams added.

"Well, that happens when you turn your back to the true lineage of our Lord Jesus Christ, the Word of God. They have misinterpreted the Bible and now the blind leads the blind. It's a shame, but what can be done? It is known that since Peter the Apostle lead the first church to now, we have been the true lineage of the Christian Faith and we do recognize when God has blessed us with an opportunity, we have the right to receive with humble appreciation."

"Religion has always been a deterrent for mankind." President Fischer stated.

"On the contrary, my dear President, it is ignorance that has been a great deterrent of human growth. All these Christians of different denominations come out of ignorance. But I think that by enforcing the Chip throughout the world that we shall find less ignorance and more enlightened minds in the world." The Cardinal as always spoke with a smile. "I am tired of these so called Christians that constantly are looking at the Vatican as we are some form of money hungry Anti-Christ, it's absurd!"

"Well unless these Christians organizations change their minds, they are about to enter into a very difficult time." Prime Minister Williams added.

"The President of Italy was not able to accompany us today. But I assure you Cardinal that as of now Europe and the United States, are well on their way to a Bio-Chip society and very soon, thanks to the Vatican, Central and South America completely will join us. The Christians will either have to come to their senses or their cross will be too hard to bear."

Back at the dessert in Arizona under the starry night as thousands of Christian celebrate their unity and their faith in Jesus Christ, a sound of thunder was heard approaching and a cloud of dust from the distance. From far away trucks belonging to the National Guard were speeding towards the place of the Christian reunion, interrupting the assembly. Everyone looked around and they saw themselves surrounded by soldiers of the National Guard. Blinding spot lights were shined on the Christians as a voice was heard over the loud speaker, "Ladies and gentleman, you are on U.S. grounds and are to abide by the laws of the country. At this point you are breaking the Martial Law that was placed across the nation for your protection, by having this assembly!"

Some Christians tried to run away but they were knocked down to the ground. Others were frozen with fear.

"We will not arrest or punish everyone. We want the leaders of the assembly." Spoke the strong, scratchy voice of the Lieutenant leading the convoy.

Pastor Wilkinson spoke up from the front of the assembly, "I am the head of this congregation."

Then the other leaders of different Christian Denominations began to yell out, "No, I am the leader!"

The Lieutenant yelled out, "Alright! Alright! I see what you are doing. It's very admirable. Ok, all of you that claim that you are leaders, line-up in the front."

Soldiers were all around standing with rifles. There were twelve male Christians that claimed that they were leaders and they were lined-up in front of the crowd. The Lieutenant looked at the soldiers surrounding the Christians and the soldiers pointed their rifles to the air and shot once. This intimidated the Christians as they fell to the ground covering their heads. Many women, children and men began to cry and tremble.

When Pastor Wilkinson saw that the crowd was being intimidated by the soldiers, something came over him and he picked up the micro-phone and started to speak.

"The Lord is my Shepherd."

When the Lieutenant saw the Pastor residing the Psalm, he ordered him to be quiet.

"I shall not want."

When the Lieutenant saw that the Pastor would not stop, he yelled louder to be quiet. But the other pastors joined in unison with Pastor Wilkinson reciting the Psalm.

"He maketh me to lie down in green pastures.

He leadeth me beside the still waters."

The people in the crowd then joined in and there were thousands of people in unison residing Psalm 23.

"He restoreth my soul; He leadeth me in the paths of righteousness for his name sake."

The Lieutenant stood in front of Pastor Wilkinson and ordered him to stop.

"Stop now!" He yelled as he got close to the Pastor's face.

They all continued in unison, "Yea, though I walk through the Valley of the Shadow of Death, I will fear no evil."

As they said these words the Lieutenant took out a stick, "Ok, so be it!"

He gave the signal to the other soldiers and they started to beat the twelve men in front of the crowd. Hitting them on the head, legs, and arms as they covered their face and anywhere else the sticks would hit.

"For though art with me; thy rod and thy staff they comfort me."

As the twelve leaders were beaten with the sticks, they never stopped residing Psalm 23 and the crowd with them.

"Thou preparest a table before me in the presence of mine enemies."

People in the crowd were crying, but they would not stop residing the Psalm. The twelve leaders were being beaten, but as they bled, they would not stop saying the psalm.

"Thou annointest my head with oil; my cup runneth over."

As they were saying these words the Lieutenant looked at Pastor Wilkinson and he realized that he was dead and his blood was all over his shoes. He looked at the lifeless body and felt anger.

As he turned around to the crowd he yelled, "What's wrong with you people? You are a bunch of crazy fanatics! This is not a game! This is for real and sooner or later you will die if you don't stop!" He yelled at the crowed. But they paid no mind, as they continued the Psalm.

"This will stand as your final warning. If you form any congregation, you will be arrested or worse! Stop it!" The Lieutenant signaled his men to go.

"Surely, goodness and mercy shall follow me all the days of my life."

As they were saying this all the other soldiers surrounded the Christians and they started to walk into the crowds and randomly started to hit people. Some people moved and others started backing away. But they all continued reciting the Psalm. There was blood everywhere and the people began to run away. But many noticed that some of the leaders were not moving.

"And I will dwell in the house of the Lord forever. Amen."

Later that night they found that three of the twelve leaders had died, including Pastor Wilkinson. The other nine were all in critical conditions, along with three-hundred people from the crowd that were either in critical condition or with minor problems. The echo of thousands of people reciting Psalm 23 was left in the warm breeze of the desserts of Arizona as a supplication for God, to have mercy on his people.

CHAPTER EIGHTEEN

Tribulations

The incident at Yuma, Arizona was a life changing experience for numerous Christians. Many Believers after watching the news felt fear and surprise that the government was taking such harsh measurements against them; they felt as if they had no strong leadership. Everyone was questioning the probability that the Anti-Christ was actually in the world, it seemed insane. Christians felt that there was not enough evidence for the amount of panic and punishment that was being experienced. Was the Bio-chip a Satanical manipulation or was it just a physiological invasion brought on by an entrepreneur to become richer? A great deal of Christians felt that if the Bio-chip was Satanical and it was part of Satan's scheme to take over God's creation; if indeed, it was the dawn of the prophecies of Revelation, then God needed to guide his people.

Confusion and doubt was beginning to grow among a great deal of Christians and they wanted to do what was right in God's eyes. But they also loved their country and they wanted to stand by their government. They wanted to be respectful American citizens. Even Jesus expressed the idea that we are to "Render Cesar what is Cesar's and God what is God's". But had we reached a point in the history of our society where the conflict between Church and State was unrepairable? Some asked the question if this was part of the Anti-Christ plan, to create a wall between the Government and God's people, creating a situation like that of Israel and Egypt during the time of Moses. There was endless amount of questions and even more confusion. Many Christians chose to make peace with their country, and do what the government asked of them; believing that they will continue in their faith.

Joseph was a tall, strong, southern Afro-American from Virginia and a survivor from the incident at Yuma, Arizona.

When the crowd dispersed a group of about twenty-five people helped each other to escape and were able to find refuge behind a rocky area where they sat to rest.

"I can't believe what I saw with my own eyes." Joseph spoke with a heavy Virginian accent.

Everyone was trying to calm down, as they felt over-powered by their adrenaline.

"It is time to start believing. It is time to realize that the Unholy Trinity has embarked on their attack on human nature." John spoke clearly as if in a trance.

"The Unholy Trinity?" Miriam, a young Puerto Rican woman from the Bronx, NY asked with concern. "I have heard of the Holy Trinity. What are you talking about?" She spoke English with a mix Spanish-Bronx Puerto Rican accent.

"The Unholy Trinity is the combination of Satan, The Anti-Christ and the False Prophet." Pastor Wilson from Oklahoma explained.

"What are we supposed to do?" A young man named Leo from California asked.

Pastor Wilson answered, "Pastor Wilkinson was right, we must pray and rest in God with faith. We must plan to help each other and other Christians across the country."

"This is crap! Faith, love and scripture do not help when real bullets are being shot at our heads." A young man from Arizona spoke up, "I am out of here and I am going back home. Tomorrow I will go and do what my Government wants me to do and try to get back to a normal life." As the young man said this a few people left with him.

"Pastor, what are you doing?" Michael asked. "You asked me to come to the meeting and wait. I did. I have to concern myself with my wife and baby. We do not know anything for sure and the answers are creating more confusion. Deborah and I are going home and we are following the government's order."

"Okay, my son. I am sorry I failed you." Pastor Silva answered.

"You did not fail us, Pastor," Deborah answered.

"I failed to provide guidance," The Pastor explained.

"One day all this shall pass. Maybe it's not as bad as we are making it." Deborah was tired. She was trying to convince herself with her own words.

After Michael and Deborah left there was twelve people left.

"Our only hope," Joseph spoke up, "Is to create an underground web to help ourselves and other Christians around the country."

"What is your name?" John asked him.

"Joseph Fluellin, sir." The man from Virginia answered.

"Well, Joseph, prepare yourself, for God has great plans for you. He has great plans for all of us. And He has brought us together." John spoke up.

"It is obvious that the authorities and the government are serious. We have to create a reliable way for us and other Christians across the country to survive." Pastor Wilson explained.

An Afro-American woman from Georgia named Millie spoke up, "On my phone there was news that in Mississippi a church gathered to pray. The National Guard broke into the church and arrested the Pastor. He had removed the boards that the soldiers had placed at the church doors. Some of the Christian men fought back to help the Pastor and in the process things got out of control and five people were killed."

"My God," Miriam gasped.

"We are going to see more and more of this not only in the United States, but all around the world." Explained Pastor Silva.

"It's beginning to happen. All around the world people will die in the name of Jesus." Pastor Wilson added.

"Are these the Martyrs that are spoken of in the Bible?" Millie asked.

"There will be many more throughout the period of the reign of the Anti-Christ." Pastor Wilson explained.

"That is sad," Miriam almost whispered.

Pastor Wilson spoke up, "My Brothers, there are twelve of us in this group. As I listen to you, I realize that we are all from different parts of the nation. There were twelve sons to Jacob, who became Israel and then they went on to become the twelve tribes of Israel. When our Lord Jesus Christ was on earth, he had twelve apostles, which after Jesus was crucified they went on to change the world. Tonight there are twelve of us and the Lord has put in my heart that we must go back to our homes and stay in touch with each other; that we must spread the word to Christians in the United States and abroad that we will help all Christians to survive this time of tribulation. We need to help each other to create an underground Christian world that will help us to supply us with our needs, to help those in need. We need Christian doctors, Christian computer experts, Christian truck drivers and Christians in all walks of life to fight this war. We will need canned food, water and medication. We must go back and make Christians around the globe realize, that this is not our world. But with the power of faith and a desire to help one another, we will see the "Amazing Grace" of God materialize before us. And most of all pray, pray and pray."

The twelve put themselves in a circle and held hands to pray, aware of the fact that their lives' were forever changed.

Deborah and Michael walked quickly behind a few bushes trying to reach the parked cars without being noticed. There were police cars everywhere and people scattered all over the place. Someone had the idea of shutting off the generators and the place was dark. The police had no interest in arresting, but they wanted to make sure that the Christians were scared. In the process they were hurting people physically. Everywhere there was police officers standing over someone and beating them.

Over the loud speaker you heard the Lieutenant, "Please, tonight go back to your homes and inform your family and friends to respect the Martial Law. You are not supposed to congregate. If you had respected the Martial Law that was placed by your President, this never would have occurred."

Deborah and Michael looked around with disbelief as they lay under a car. They feared for their life. Michael was very scared that Deborah would lose the baby.

"Do you know where our car is?" Michael whispered to Deborah, making sure no one would hear him.

"Yes, I have an idea." Deborah answered.

"You have to go. Keep going under the cars and there is less of a chance of someone spotting you. The two of us together is dangerous." Michael tried to explain.

"No! Together! We go together and stay together!" Deborah insisted.

"This is no time for you to be stubborn! Keep going to the car and stay down, when you see the first chance to leave safely, you go!" Michael insisted.

"No! Come with me!" Deborah fought back.

"Think of the baby!" Michael argued.

"I will think of the baby and you. We are a family!" Deborah argued.

"If they find us and hit you the wrong way, you could lose the baby." Michael pleaded.

"Together!" Deborah said firmly.

"Okay. But we need to move." Michael said giving up the argument.

In the meantime there was a lot of scrambling around in the dust as people were trying to get in their cars to drive away. Deborah noticed that if people drove away the police would let them go; the problem was if they caught the person before they got into the car. Deborah and Michael reached their car and as Deborah got in the car and turned it on a soldier grabbed Michael by the legs and pulled him from under the car. Deborah started to scream as Michael yelled, "Go! Go! Drive away!"

"Michael!" Deborah yelled back.

At that point Deborah realized that there was a soldier standing by the window tapping the glass with his stick.

"Open the window!" He said firmly.

Deborah looked back and realized that Michael was not there. They had taken him. She put the car on "D" and pressed on the accelerator to take off. As she drove, she kept looking on the rearview mirror and saw only dust. She got on the main road and speeded away. As she held tightly onto the steering wheel, she noticed that no one was following her. Deborah drove and cried. She prayed to God to help her and Michael. She thought about the baby and she was scared. She decided then and there, that she was going to get the Biochip. She wanted a normal life for her baby, and she wanted Michael back.

"I am sorry, God. But you are asking too much of me. Please help me! Please!" Deborah prayed as she drove away.

CHAPTER NINTEEN

Rising Above

In front of the White House there were about five-hundred very angry people from all over the country. There were people with signs against the Biochip, who were not Christians, but they did not agree with having a foreign object placed in their body. They believed the Biochip to be an invasion of personal space. Many people did not appreciate the way that the government was trying to manipulate them and how, the American way of life had slowly evaporated within a series of events. People felt they needed to stand up to the government and be America, before this situation worsened. The government had done very little to help with the victims of the natural disasters that basically transformed the geographical look of the country and the spirit of the nation. There was no money to help the people that lost their homes or lands, the children that lost their parents, the broken lives or families suffering. The government had basically left the people to survive on their own, as they announced that the National Deficit was too big and there was no money to help. Millionaires were taking their money and investments out of the United States and moving it to foreign banks. The money was not there to help these people in need.

The President stood at the window of the White House, looking at the crowd at the other side of the fence. He heard their yelling.

"No Biochip!"

"Help rebuild and fix our homes!"

"No help...no taxes!"

People with microphones were yelling out.

The President listened and watched intensely. He was angry.

The President was quiet and still as a serpent before he is about to attack.

Half hour later there were hundreds of National Guard soldiers dressed in black, with helmets, shields, bullet prove vests, sticks and guns walking in perfect unison towards the crowd. A helicopter flew overhead as a speaker demanded to surrender their campaign and go home. The people through rocks at the helicopter and yelled in unison, "That they demanded changes!"

The soldiers got closer to the crowds and they started to push into the people with their shields. The sticks were taken out and they started to hit people with the sticks. People were getting hit on the head, bodies and legs. Some fell to the ground and the crowd began to push back towards the soldiers. People were getting stepped on, as they began to yell and scream. Then one person from the crowd took out a gun and shot at one of the soldiers. When the shot was heard people screamed and began to stampede; screaming and running all over the place in total chaos. The soldiers took out their guns as tear gas was shot into the crowd. There were more bullet shots heard, but it was unknown from which group or who, if anyone, was a victim. People were being stepped on as others ran away. The soldiers were beating people with their sticks and some soldiers even shot people that were trying to get aggressive with them. It was a massive chaotic blood bath.

In New York a group of over a thousand people gathered on Fifth Ave. and 33rd street with the intention to march down Fifth Ave. all the way to Central Park, jamming the traffic and making it difficult for the businesses down Fifth Ave. The television cameras were observing everything like a sponge. People were taking the opportunity to speak up in front of the cameras to entice the rest of the nation to fight back.

People would look into the camera and yelled out, "No respect for Martial Law!"

"America is for the people, by the people!"

"No, Biochip! No, Biochip!"

"Impeachment! Impeachment!"

THE TIME HAS COME

The news commentator grabbed the attention of a young man that was walking with the crowd carrying signs and chanting.

"Is there anything you want to say to our viewers?" The commentator asked.

"Yes. We are not a bunch of nuts out here with nothing to do. I am a student at NYU – Political Science and we are very serious. What are they going to do kill everyone in the country? I am not a Christian. Actually I am an atheist and proud. But when I see people in America losing their rights to practice freedom of religion. I am baffled! When I see a group of people being stripped of their Constitutional rights, I am very concerned and I ask myself, what next? Who is the next group that will lose their Constitutional Rights? We are not here for a Christian movement, we are here to preserve the Constitution of the United States!"

"What about the Biochip? Will you get the Biochip and if you don't, how will you survive?" The commentator asked.

"This is my message to the President and his Biochip..." As the young man was saying this he put his middle finger up in front of the camera. "I salute you, Mr. President!" The young man walked away and continued with the multitude, who were now yelling, "There is strength in union! There is strength in union!"

The Commentator looked at the camera and spoke into the eyes and heart of every viewer, "America is watching, Mr. President. America is speaking loudly to you and they are letting you know that your Martial Law is unconstitutional and unacceptable! We hope you are listening! America is saying enough!"

As the crowd continued walking down Fifth Ave, they were surprised when they reached 50th St. and there was thousands of National Guards and police officers dressed with their protective gear walking towards them. They wasted no time to shoot tear gas and real shots in the air to scare the crowd. Many stood their ground, but many were scared and ran for cover. A stampede immerged from the crowd and there were too many people. The stampede was lethal. People were tripping and falling on the floor. While some protesters through anything they could find at the soldiers and officers marching towards them. A couple of young protesters, thinking that they were smart, fought back by throwing a couple of bottles filled with gasoline and a rag on flames wrapped around them. When the bottles hit the streets they shattered and as the gasoline spread all over the street so did the flames, burning many officers. This inflamed the soldiers and the officers with anger and they began to shoot into the crowd. People ran as bullets flew and killed. People were being hurt and killed by the bullets, the blinding smoke bombs, tripping and the stampede. Many died that day and many more were hurt. But most importantly America's Citizens understood that their country was not same.

Later that day the President addressed the nation. Sitting in the Oval Office he looked into the camera, "My fellow Americans today is a very sad day in the history of this country. With the incident at Yuma, Arizona and Washington, D.C., and New York it saddens me to see that some Americans are failing to understand that progression is a way of life. I suggest to everyone that you comply with the order of the Biochip. Our nation, like Europe, will be running with a modern technological system that if you do not have the Biochip you will not be able to use your finances or even buy anything. It will be a very unnecessarily uncomfortable situation for you.

I know that our country has needs caused by natural disasters and I assure you that those needs will be met accordingly. We are on a tremendous financial difficulty; aware of the fact that many entrepreneurs have taken their finances out of American banks. These people do not feel secure enough to invest in our country. Our government is working with them to come up with a secure solution in order for them to feel safe again to invest within our country. Everyone wants to resolve this situation. Once this problem is fixed, we shall be able to accommodate the needs of the citizens of this country caused by the natural disaster we have endured. I ask you to be patient. I ask you to trust and work with your country, not against it. And I apologize to the many, for the sins of the few, for the Martial Law will not be lifted until we feel safe in our country. It is for the protection of every citizen. We Americans always rise above whatever situation may challenge us. Good night and God bless you."

CHAPTER TWENTY

I Am Here

The limousine pulled up next to the Bellevue Palace, home of President Fischer in Germany. The President walked with a couple of his agents to the door of the limousine, as one of the guards opened the door he got inside and was greeted by The Voice.

"I felt it was time to pay you a visit," The Voice began, as he sat in a dark corner of the limousine and Fischer was only able to see the lower part of The Voice's body.

President Fischer smiled, "I have done so much for you and I am part of your Illuminated Dark Society, you don't feel comfortable with me knowing your identity?"

"It has nothing to do with my comfort. For now, it is important that we do things this way. Do not get *comfortable,* President Fischer. We still have a lot of work to do. We have a lot of enemies and I feel more confident knowing that if you get kidnapped, you will not disclose my identity and believe me when I tell you, you don't want to know who I am." The Voice spoke firmly.

"Let's talk about Europe." The Voice changed the subject.

"Europe is under our control; recuperating from the pass, flourishing, enjoying a peaceful life. The majority of the people in Europe are feeling at peace, as they work and enjoy life. The Biochip has been a total success. Except for some insignificant small group of people, trying to create complications and of course the Christians, life has never been so good and productive in Europe. The Intelligent Service of Europe (ISE) have done a great job in keeping order. Everyone is watching us and we are a success." Fischer spoke with pride.

"I am glad to hear your description of our European project. You have done an outstanding job, but your tone worries me. Do not make your confidence your weakness. We must stay on top of the Christians. If Non-Christians do not want the Biochip, let them suffer to their heart's content. But if Christians do not want the BioChip, make sure you make them suffer and make it difficult for them to survive."

"Why do you have a vendetta against the Christians?" Fischer asked.

"It's not a vendetta. The Christians have faith and faith creates strength and the combination of faith and strength create motivation. Motivated Christians are a problem that could only be resolved by terminating them. So, we need to discourage them before we have to terminate them." Fischer looked at the dark figure of The Voice with fear.

Fischer asked, "What if the view the Christians have of God, is correct? Does it concern you?"

The Voice answered, "It is correct and that is precisely why I will terminate them."

Fischer looked at The Voice afraid to annunciate his next question, "Are you the...the Anti-Christ?"

"I am," The Voice answered. "I am here."

Fischer's mouth became dry and he had never felt so much fear in his life. "Remember Fischer, you are mine. Do not weaken like Prime Minister Taylor and create a similar destiny as his."

He did not want to know anymore, keeping calm he changed the conversation.

"What about the Vatican?" Fischer asked.

"The Vatican is my pride. Through the Vatican I have acquired the trust of Russia, Spain, Mexico, countries in South America that blindly follow the Pope and he has become, not my Pope, but my Prophet. He is a beacon that lights on top of the mountain and the blind follow the light like flies to their doom. Ignorance is my greatest ally and the masses, must believe that I am not here. That I don't exist as they follow my pride, my prophet." The Voice spoke with conviction.

"Is everything under control in the United States?" Fischer asked.

"The United States has been a bigger challenge than Europe. But that is more of a problem for their citizens than it is for our plan. President Paraish is solid with the Illuminated minds of our Dark Society. He understands how he got there and where his loyalty belongs." The Voice explained.

"Are they going to maintain the Martial Law?" Fischer asked.

"Paraish has Congress in his pocket. We have made sure of that. No one in Congress will make a move to remove the Martial Law. The National Guard, plus all other branches of the United States Arm Forces have every active soldier at home actively guarding the country. I spoke to Paraish and we set a dead line for citizens to get their Biochip. If they don't by the deadline, they will be considered criminals in the United States for insubordination and treason. Bounty hunters will be rewarded for seeking and finding these criminals." The Voice explained.

"It's not just Christians, is it?" Fischer asked.

"No. They have citizens who do not believe in the Biochip and in doing so, they have ruined their lives." The Voice explained.

"The Christians in the United States will give us a fight. I know that they will prepare some form of clandestine covert operation to protect Christians and to make sure they have shelter and food. But Paraish will seek them out and at that time we will give them a chance to turn to us or die." The Voice spoke coldly.

"I am sure many will die." Fischer said softly as he thought about religious fanatics. He never had time for God or religion and founded amazing how people are willing to die for their faith.

"That will be their choice. I have Paraish communicating with President Raashida of Israel." The Vice Stated.

"Israel?" Fischer was surprised.

"President Raashida has accepted the Biochip and of course has realized how lucrative it could be for Israel in these times of changes. Israel has joined us without a problem." The Voice explained.

"I was amazed when the Muslims moved to other areas of the Middle East and left the land of Jerusalem to the Israelites. Did you have something to do with that?" Fischer asked.

"Don't worry, the Muslim world have received their long awaited Calif and they are now united and Muslims from all over the world are traveling to Syria to meet and be taught directly by their Prophet, The Calif. They are going to be known as The United Muslim-Arab World. At the same time the Israelites will begin to build their third Temple with jubilee. They will be allowed to build their Temple and to enjoy their land. But nothing is forever, my friend, for when death comes knocking at the door, it all crumbles down."

"Congratulations, it seems like you have the world in your hands. What about the rest of the world?" Fischer asked.

"Pestilence, diseases, death, natural disasters, it will be quite a show; so much destruction that it won't even be worth it to me to waste my time with those people." The Voice spoke coldly.

Fischer watched with fear.

"Why me? Why do you give me the honor of controlling Europe for you?" Fischer asked.

"I owe it to you ancestor. I placed in your hands, what Hitler worked so hard for and failed. Don't fail me. You are there because I know that your heart is as cold as mine. You can have what you want, but do not go insane. Insanity will destroy your power. I have made many leaders throughout history go insane, when I didn't need them anymore. Stay sharp for you are one of my kings." The Voice spoke boldly.

Fischer left the limousine feeling like a giant with weak knees. He was not sure if to say, thank-you; or if to run like hell. But he knew that now there was no way out. There was no turning back, no matter how scary it may be. Destiny had brought us to this point in history and we all had to swallow, no matter how bitter. Fischer was ready to be the "king" of Europe.

The Voice picked up his phone in the limousine and placed a called to Syria.

"Hello." The Calif answered the phone.

"Hello, my friend. How are you?" The Voice asked.

"All things in place, the United Muslim-Arab World of Islam is in full force. Muslims are coming from all over the world and we are more united than ever. Every one of us has accepted the Biochip as a gift from Allah himself and we are ready to embark into a new time in history." The Calif spoke.

The Voice spoke freely to the Calif, "I knew that I could count with you. I know that I could always count on you, my Prophet, my friend. Guide and teach these people. We already have placed the World Bank in order and the Bio-chip. Soon we will have a World Religion and my prophets will be there with me."

"Our goal will materialize in time." The Calif assured The Voice.

"I will visit you soon." The Voice continued. "I long to see Syria my true homeland. Remember only you know about my mother, she was a Syrian woman and people wanted to take me from her. She escaped to family she had living in Bosnia, to give birth to me safely, away from those who wanted to take me. But the poor woman did not understand my destiny, and the men found her the night of my birth and killed her. I am the prophecy; I am here."

"The time has come, my friend." The Calif agreed.

CHAPTER TWENTY-ONE

Be Still And Know That I Am God

John slowly walked into the cold, concrete and glass government building. He opened the heavy glass door as he walked towards the metal detector where three guards, without expression, stood with rifles. John put his belongings in a basket on the rail along with his long black coat. After walking through the metal detector one of the guards scanned a hand held metal detector over his body, even though he did not set off any alarms.

John handed the letter from the United States Government to the guard as he grabbed his belongings.

"Go through that door." The guard commanded.

John took the letter back and headed towards the door. He slowly opened the door and found a room full of people speaking softly to each other; people from all walks of life. They were all types of ages, race and status. Some people seem confused, some excited and some scared. John looked around and felt sad that he was only there for one person.

As he looked towards the front of the lines, he found Deborah standing two people away from reaching an agent. John slowly walked up to her, trying to not create a scene. When Deborah looked up she gasped.

"John, what are you doing here?" she asked.

John spoke slowly, "Don't do this, Deborah. Come with me. Have faith; you will be fine."

Jill standing behind Deborah looked at John, "Deborah, you know this guy? Is he bothering you?"

Deborah looked at John and hugged her stomach as she spoke, "No, it's okay, Jill. He is leaving now."

Deborah's eyes watered as she said this.

"Deborah, we have doctors that are joining our movement and will help you deliver your baby. It won't cost you a thing.

We will all help one another. But please don't do this." John insisted.

"Oh, I get it," Jill jumped in, "this is one of your Christian friends. Deborah, don't listen to him. Think about your baby. Mister, you have a nerve coming in here!"

Deborah looked at John, "John, I know you are here because you care about me." She smiled at him as tears came down her face. "But Michael is dead. What am I supposed to do? I have to raise my baby by myself. I don't have the right to raise him in a normal life? Normal! I don't want my baby to be chased or to live hiding underground because he is a Christian. I don't want him to be a reject in our society. I want the best for my baby. If that makes me a bad person, then I am a bad person. So be it."

"You are afraid because of the baby. I understand that. But you know in your heart, that if you want the best for your baby... your faith in Jesus is what's best for him. Please don't let go of that beautiful sincere faith you have. Just be still and know that he is God. Let him do his work." John pleaded.

"That's just it," Deborah spoke slowly, "Maybe I don't have faith anymore. Maybe God waited too long to help me. I no longer feel that commitment to Jesus; that first love or joy. I don't know. My commitment is to my baby." Deborah looked into John's eyes as she asked him, "Why did God fail me, John?"

Jill jumped in, "Take care of your baby. Don't let anyone tell you what to do. Listen to your heart!"

John looked at Jill, "Like you listened to your heart when your brother was trying to keep you from coming here?"

Jill's face became pale and she felt a chill as she asked John, "Who are you. What do you know about me or my brother?"

"I don't know anything about you, but God knows you, your brother and your family. Your brother is a Christian and he tried to prevent you from coming here." John stated emphatically.

Jill's forehead wrinkled as she looked at John and then looked around unsure of what to make of John's words.

"Deborah, please," John said softly.

The lady at the window yelled, "Next."

Deborah walked towards the window as she looked at John, "I am sorry it has to be this way. I love you guys."

John watched Deborah walk towards the window, where the lady waited to insert the Micro-Bio Chip in Deborah's hand. John turned around and walked away.

Pastor Silva and Yannel were having a *cafezinho* and talking to each other as they watched the news.

"I guess I shall never return to Israel," Yannel said sadly.

"Never say, that you will never go back to Israel, my friend. As immigrants we do not know where tomorrow will take us." Pastor Silva spoke encouragingly.

"I felt different than they did. I felt that I should have been happy for my people. Instead I felt a strong feeling to warn them. I felt that everything that was happening was a big warning sign of something horrible that will happen. No one will listen; it's destiny." Yanel spoke with frustration.

"There are many warning signs, my brother; warning signs that we may or may not observe. You are a Christian and the best thing that you could do for yourself and for your family is to pay attention to the signs that God gives you. It is frustrating because even though, we may see and understand certain things, it does not mean that we will be able to make others understand. People understand religion, but not faith. God gave us faith, religion was created by man." Pastor Silva spoke with sadness.

As Yanel picked up the *cafezinho* the newscaster began to speak about international news.

"Today in Israel," The newscaster reported, "The Jewish people continue to celebrate their homeland after sharing the land for so many years with the Muslims. A Muslim decision that has surprised the entire world after their Calif has arrived, Muslims throughout the world have migrated to Syria where they are being taught and guided by the Calif himself. The Jewish community has begun to build their temple after so many years of not having one. The Temple will be built in conjunction with the Western Wall which was part of the old Jewish Temple before it was destroyed. It will take three and a half years to build according to plans. The Jewish community and the Muslim community have both accepted to be part of the Micro-bio Chip and feel that it will be lucrative, as well as good for the people."

"You hear that?" Yanel asked Pastor Silva.

"It is done, my friend," Pastor Silva answered.

"Many will die," Yanel stated.

"They will wait for them to build the temple. In three and a half years the Anti-Christ will betray the Israelites. He will forget the "peace treaty" and as the Jewish people continue in their prosperity and jubilation the Anti-Christ will massacre them with a surprise attack. He will live in the Temple built by the Jews and will allow the Muslims to go back to Jerusalem."

"There is nothing that could be done." Yanel stated.

"It is as the prophesy states." Pastor Silva explained.

"It is sad," Yanel concluded.

In a remote area in Syria millions of Muslims have united in silence and prayer. Muslims from all over the world as well as the Middle East are all gathered in front of the Calif. The awaited one, that was to bring together the Muslim world. No longer would there be divisions between Shiites, Sunnis or any other form of groups of the Islamic-Arab world. Now they had peace and would follow only the guidance and leadership of the one chosen by Allah. Now it was the dawn of a different life and the Calif walked with his robe in front of the millions that were on their knees with their heads bowed to the ground before him.

Everyone was in perfect silence as the Calif spoke, "For many years we have been divided. For many years we suffered the insults of the Western World and the degrading mentality of Judaism and Christianity towards the true God, Allah. For many years our brothers have run around doing atrocities in the name of Allah that has shamed our teachings. Now it all comes to an end. As of today, anyone that takes it upon himself to act in the name of Allah without the consent of "The United Muslim-Arab World" will be considered a traitor and blasphemy before Allah and will be punished only by death. My brothers, we have accepted the Micro-Biochip as a sign that the old world has joined the new and that "The United Muslim-Arab World" will not give into the ways of the new "World Government", but that the new "World Government" will respect "The United Muslim-Arab World"; and in turn it will be a very lucrative time for our people."

As the Calif concluded his speech and stood in silence, the millions continued with their heads bowed to the ground and praying silently with outmost respect.

Pastor Silva and Yanel continued to watch the news as they rested in Pastor Silva's house. There was a knock on the door and it was John.

"Hi, John, come in." Pastor Silva looked at John and asked, "Are you okay?" Pastor Silva asked as John walked in.

John seemed quiet and very distraught.

"Would you like some water?" The Pastor asked.

"Yes, thank you." John answered absentmindedly.

"Hello, John," Yanel said happily to see his old friend.

"Hello, Yanel. It's so good to see you. I have been worried about you." John said with a smile.

They both shook hands and hugged as they smiled at each other.

"I am very happy to see you too. But you seem very preoccupied." Yanel was sincerely concerned.

"What do we know about Michael?" John asked as he looked at Pastor Silva's eyes.

"Michael is missing?" Yanel asked.

"Last time I saw Michael and Deborah was at Yuma." The Pastor answered.

"I knew in my heart, Deborah was going to go to the government building to get the Biochip as soon as she got back from Arizona. I went there and used my letter to get in, to try to talk her out of it. To my surprise she is under the impression that Michael got killed. She feels that now more than ever she needs the Biochip because she has to raise the baby alone. But do we know if Michael is dead?" John explained.

Pastor Silva taking out his cell phone stated, "I will call his cell phone."

"Deborah is getting the Biochip?" Yanel asked.

"Yeah, I was not able to change her mind." John answered.

"No answer," Pastor Silva confirmed.

"It's hard for me to believe that if Deborah got the Biochip that God will condemn her. Her faith is very honest. It would be a shame." Yanel stated.

"Deborah has been through a lot. She feels that God has abandoned her. She is thinking about her baby. She is thinking with her natural mother instincts." John explained.

"God works in mysterious ways. Ways that it would be impossible for us to understand. It will be very difficult for us to be able to have an underground Christian organization if we do not have people with the Biochip helping us." Pastor Silva explained.

"God chooses different Christians for different works. Not all Christians are Pastors, or preachers, or singers and as a Christian we all have to develop our destiny with God. Maybe the same way we know that there will be Martyrs, the Exile and the 144,000 etc.; people from the end times. I think that there will be a few chosen people that even though they have the Biochip, they will have a decision to make. If the Holy Spirit moves them to help the Christians and they do, they will be recompensed. But if they are afraid and refuse to follow their Christian instincts then they will be condemned."

"So, then why don't all the Christians just get the Biochip?" Yanel asked.

"Unless you have been chosen by God to this for him, the Holy Spirit will not be with you. It's like trying to be part of a chorus when God has not given you the gift of singing." Pastor Silva explained.

"Also, it seems easy, but it's not. The people that are chosen by God to get the Biochip and help the Christians are going to live very dangerous lives. They will have to have a very strong faith and mentality. It won't be easy because they will constantly be living breaking the law of the land and trying not to get caught." John added.

"We will have a very difficult job with the Underground Christian Organization. We will need a lot of help. I hope people like Deborah remember us." Pastor Silva stated.

"I hope God remembers people like Deborah." John spoke softly.

As the three friends were speaking to each other a "Special Report" came on the news. All three listened attentively to the commentator, "Different countries like India, China, Japan and other parts of the Eastern World, as well as countries throughout Africa are suffering from the worst cases of deadly viruses known in the history of mankind. Some viruses have symptoms of rashes and soars throughout the body that itch and hurt. Some virus' symptoms are fever and are unable to hold anything in the stomach. Scientists have no idea if the viruses are spreading with mosquitoes or other insects. There is one virus that causes different parts of the body to swell. People have choked to death as their throat swells to the point that they can't breathe. All the viruses are very contagious. The death toll is unknown, but it constantly increases during the day."

As the reporter spoke the cameras were showing scenes from affected areas. Countries filled with pestilences and sickness. The cameras showed adults and children laying down on small beds as they coughed and slowly wasted away to death; people in China, Japan, India and The Philippines dropping dead on the streets.

"Some doctors believe," the reporter continued, "that some of the viruses are airborne and people throughout these countries are encouraged to wear masks. Doctors are doing everything possible to help, but the fight is so impossible because doctors and nurses are literally dropping dead to the floor as they try to help patience."

The reporter continued, "The New World Government forming throughout Europe, North and South America, and Australia have not been affected by any of the viruses. Many are surprised that the Middle East, Syria, Saudi Arabia, Iraq and all the other countries joining as one in The United Muslim-Arab World have not suffered any consequences due to these mysterious viruses."

The newscaster continued to speak into the camera, "The world is going through a very confusing time, for even though, we have to face natural disasters like viruses, earthquakes and other natural phenomena the world has never seemed as together as we are now. The new "World Government", the Biochip, The United Muslim-Arab World, have all accomplished what no other world leader in history has been able to accomplish, World Peace and Unification. This is a miracle not only in Israel, but in the Middle East, Europe, North and South America, as well as the rest of the world."

"It is ironic to think that the group that throughout the times have always spoken about love and faith as being the core of their beliefs, is the one group that find themselves against the Biochip and at war with all the changes occurring in the world. Their view is that there is only one man behind the changes that has occurred in the world and that is the Anti-Christ. The Christians also believe the Biochip is the same as the 'number of the beast' as it is referred to in the Book of Revelations in The Bible. Now the Vatican and the Catholics who follow the same Bible have welcomed the Biochip and the changes as a blessing. We hope that the millions of Christians that are suffering unnecessarily would come to their senses and realize that this man, they call The Anti-Christ, has been able to do for the world what Jesus Christ, Gandhi, Buddha and even Martin Luther King, Jr. only dreamed of. One man who has made a new world government, a world bank, a world solidification, and world peace all on his own does not sound like the work of an Anti-Christ."

"Well there you have it," John spoke as the report concluded, "like an angel of light the Anti-Christ, the right hand of Satan, will come and mislead the world with lies and the world like flies will follow its beacon until they get close enough to fry. It's so sad." John put his head down and exhaled with frustration.

In a remote place in the Middle East a thin figure sits on cushioned black chair before a shiny cedar wood table. His face is thin and smooth shaven with a dark olive tan. His eyes are blue and deep as the ocean, radiating intelligence and self assurance; no fears, no worries only strength. His black hair was combed back and shiny. He wore a white suite with a white shirt, white tie and the ensemble was completed with white shoes. He looks at the group sitting in front of him and speaks in a soft voice. "You are all leaders." He begins.

"You are our Lord," They speak in unison.

The thin man looked around and watched the four men that surrounded him President Fischer, President Paraish, The Pope and The Calif.

"You are all my leaders and we are the New World Government, we are The United Arab-Muslim World, we are The Vatican, we are the illuminated minds that for centuries, since The Tower of Babel, have tried to unite the world against God, called Jehovah; the God of Abraham; the God of Israel and Christianity."

As the thin man spoke with his leaders, in Israel soldiers were chasing Christians and knocking them on the ground. Some Christians were tied up and were dragged on the streets.

"Who is your God?" They were asked.

"Who is your King?" They were mocked.

But the Christians would always answer "Jesus" and they were taken to be crucified. But the soldiers were told to crucify the Christians upside down.

"We crucify you in the name of the Anti-Christ!" As they said this the Christians were nailed to upside down crosses. As this occurred the Israelites would close the doors and windows of their houses not seeing the evil and choosing not to get involved. The blood of the Christians dried on the streets of Israel, Europe, the Americas and through all the Middle East.

Special "Christian Hunters" were prepared by the Anti-Christ to seek out the Christians in every part of the world and to give them one last chance to renounce Christ or to die crucified to an upside down cross, the cross of the Anti-Christ.

The Christians were forced to work hard and non-stop to build the "Underworld Christian Community" where there were no more denominations, only Christians that read The Bible, prayed and lived with faith and love helping one another to survive. Many Christians with the Biochip lived endangering their lives everyday helping the Christians to acquire food and basic necessities of life. Throughout the world the blood of people with a solid Christian faith was heard from the rubble of the streets crying to God for help, but willing to die for their faith in Jesus Christ.

A young woman walked into an abandoned church wearing a black long cape and a hood, carefully watching and making sure that she was not being followed and carrying three bag packs; one on her back and one on each hand. All three were heavy and loaded with can foods and other necessities. The church was full of dust and rubble. The benches and the alter were dirty with layers of dust and stones. The ceiling was full of holes and there was water from rain all over the old church that smell like mildew. The woman reached an area of the abandoned church that had a door on the floor that lead to a cellar. The woman stepped on the cellar door and stumped on it hard three times in the manner that she was told it would be a recognizable code. As she stepped back the cellar door opened and a young man asked.

"What do you want?"

"I am a Christian and I have food for all of you." She whispered.

"Are you sure you were not followed?" The man asked.

"Yes. Now let me in, hurry!" She demanded.

As she was led down the dark dusty stairs there was a group of people sitting in different areas of the cellar with little light. John, Pastor Silva and another pastor came to the young lady.

"Are you alright? Did anyone see you?" Pastor Silva asked.

"No one saw me and you have nothing to worry about. I bring you lots of food and water. I found out you were here by other Christians that have brought you things." The woman explained.

"Yes, of course and we appreciate everything you can do for us. God bless you and your family." Pastor Silva spoke very humbly.

John looked at her and asked, "What is your name? Please remove the hood."

As the woman removed her hood John and Pastor Silva found the smiling face of Deborah. "It's me, Deborah."

John smiled and hugged her warmly.

"Sorry about the last time we saw each other." Deborah said.

"So, am I; I was so scared for you, I think I was trying to fix God's plan. We could never do that. I then understood that God had his own plan for you."

"I almost ran after you at the Federal Building, but something told me not to and I acted by faith."

"How's the baby?" Pastor Silva asked.

"Great. Thank God, he is a healthy baby." Deborah answered with a smile.

"Do you know anything about Michael?" John asked.

"No," Deborah answered sadly, "but honestly, my gut tells me his alive."

"I have the same feeling," John confessed, "I honestly feel that we will find him.

"So this is the Truth? The Bible was right the whole time? This is Revelation coming to reality and The Anti-Christ now is in control?" Deborah asked.

"Yes, The Anti-Christ will rule for seven years and the Christians have finally realized that we could only fight back with faith, love, prayer and Bible. Religion has become something of the world of the Anti-Christ." John explained.

"He is now pushing for a World Religion." Deborah explained.

"He will get it, The Dead Church of the World Religion." John stated.

Deborah now seemed stronger as a person and in her faith.

"I guess we can't argue with the Prophesies," she said softly.

"The time is here!" John exclaimed.

ABOUT the AUTHOR

Alfonso Fumero
Born in Havana, Cuba. Has been studying the Bible since he was 14 years old. Has been invited to preach in various English and Spanish Christian churches throughout the years. Has made the book of Revelation his main focal point of study over the last five years. Has run youth groups, as well as Bible Classes. Works with Autistic children as well as students with other learning disabilities.

With Special Contributions From:

Eneida Dias
Born in Rio de Janeiro, Brazil. Graduated in Psychology concentrated in Jungian studies. Always involved in religious facts, attracted Revelations. She loves working in research.

www.ingramcontent.com/pod-product-compliance
Lightning Source LLC
Chambersburg PA
CBHW030618130626
46552CB00002B/621